## "I suppose I should get right down to the point of why I asked you here."

Elijah put his knife and fork down and placed his elbows on the table.

Lily nodded. "The best way to do it is to say it quickly."

"That's one of the things I like about you, Lily. You're so forthright."

"Isn't it the best way to be?"

Noticing he wasn't smiling, she no longer thought he'd brought her there to propose. Or was he simply working up the nerve to ask if they could be boyfriend and girlfriend? Surely he knew she'd be happy about that. Why was he looking so sad?

Finally, she said, "You don't have to tell me right away. I can wait. We haven't even finished dinner yet."

"It's something… It's hard for me to say."

"Just say it."

He nodded and then looked into her eyes.

"There's something you don't know about me."

A knot formed in Lily's stomach. What could it possibly be?

**Samantha Price** is a bestselling author who knew she wanted to become a writer at the age of seven, after her grandmother read her *The Tale of Peter Rabbit*. Though the adventures of Peter started Samantha on her creative journey, it is now her love of Amish culture that inspires her. Her writing is wholesome with more than a dash of sweetness. Samantha lives in a quaint Victorian cottage with three rambunctious dogs.

# AMISH LILY

## *Samantha Price*

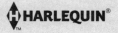

Recycling programs
for this product may
not exist in your area.

ISBN-13: 978-1-335-00603-5

Amish Lily

Copyright © 2017 by Samantha Price

This edition published by arrangement with Harlequin Books S.A.

For questions and comments about the quality of this book,
please contact us at CustomerService@Harlequin.com.

® and TM are trademarks of Harlequin Enterprises Limited or its corporate affiliates. Trademarks indicated with ® are registered in the United States Patent and Trademark Office, the Canadian Intellectual Property Office and in other countries.

**Printed in U.S.A.**

## Chapter One

Lily looked over at her twin sister, Daisy, who was staring into the eyes of Bruno as they sat at the wedding table in the yard of the family home. Most Amish weddings took place in the bride's family home and this one was no different. There were over three hundred wedding guests in the yard seated at long rows of tables, and the low buzz of many conversations was getting on Lily's nerves.

"They're sickening the way they're looking all moony-eyed at each other."

"It's not sickening," Violet said, shaking her head at Lily.

Daisy and Bruno had just gotten married and Lily tried to be happy for them, but she couldn't muster any joy. Not when Bruno was taking her twin sister away from her. She'd never been apart from her twin and they'd only ever had one large disagreement in all their years.

Lily turned back and looked across the table at her slightly younger cousins, Willow and Violet, when she heard her youngest cousin's squeaky voice.

"Don't you want to be in love someday, Lily?" Willow asked her.

"I'd have to give it some serious thought." Lily leaned closer and whispered, "Are you still going to help me with what we talked about before?"

"Were you serious about that? I told Willow you were only joking."

Lily shook her head and cackled at Violet looking so serious. "I've never been more serious."

Daisy and Bruno were staying at the Yoder family home that night, the night of their wedding, before traveling to Ohio the next day for Daisy to meet the rest of Bruno's family. From there, Bruno was taking Lily to visit other communities to see all his other relations, and then after that, they planned to stay in Ohio some more.

Lily's wicked plan was for them to short-sheet the wedding bed and, to aggravate Daisy and Bruno further, sprinkle sugar through their bed. There wouldn't be a lot of sugar—only enough so they wouldn't notice the annoyance at first. Lily thought it was a marvelous idea, and if the cousins weren't on board with it, she'd have to go solo on this one.

"Well, are you going to help me or not?" Lily stared at the cousins, wondering if they were going to be too goody-goody to help.

Violet shook her head. "I couldn't have anything to do with it. If Daisy tells your *Mamm* it might start something between our *mudders* again. They've only just started being nice to one another. And you know how Aunt Nancy can be."

Willow puffed out her chubby cheeks. "If Violet won't do it then neither will I."

Under the table, Lily's fists clenched so hard her fingernails dug into her palms. If her younger cousins listened to her they might have some fun, but they were too scared of the trouble they'd get into. She wished the cousins had never come to stay. Aunt Nerida had a broken leg and that's why Lily had been burdened with the cousins' visit, which looked as though it would be a lengthy one. Surely the girls were old enough to look after their mother and themselves. And then there was their father, Uncle John. Who was looking after him when he came home after a hard day's work? It seemed to Lily that Nerida wanted a holiday from her two girls and now Lily could see why—the two of them were as dull and boring as a gray sky on a summer's day.

Lily brightened up when she saw three young

men approaching the table. Quickly realizing the younger cousins were in the way, she knew she had to get rid of them. "You two should sit somewhere else if you're not going to follow my plans." She folded her arms and stared at Violet and Willow.

Violet drew her eyebrows together. "You don't have to be like that, Lily."

In reply, Lily spat, "Don't be so high 'n' mighty. Earlier, you thought doing all those things would be fun and you said so yourself."

"*Jah*, fun to think about, but I didn't think you would actually do it."

Willow added, "I just don't want to get into trouble."

*Boring as well as stupid*, Lily thought. "I'll do it all myself then, but don't you breathe a word of it, and don't blame me if anyone asks you. Just say you don't know anything about it. Now I need the two of you to go because I've got some boys coming this way to see me. Scat!" When they stared at her blankly, she said through gritted teeth, "Do you understand? Scram! Get!"

"Come on, Willow. She doesn't want us around."

"You got that right," Lily said under her breath.

Violet slipped her arm through her sister's and together they stood up. They walked away just as the three young men reached the table. There was nothing Lily liked better than the adoring attention the young men were giving her of late.

* * *

Nancy was happy that her third daughter was married and married to a good man, but her remaining daughter, the normally bubbly Lily, had changed into someone she didn't recognize. Now that Daisy was married, Lily was alone for the first time in her life. Daisy had her husband, but Lily, grieving from the loss of her twin, had to adjust to a totally different life—the life of a singleton. Lily had been thrust into a situation that would take some adjusting and somehow, she knew the next few months weren't going to be pleasant for her.

"Are you happy?"

Nancy looked at her husband, who was sitting next to her at one of the main wedding tables. "I am."

"We'll have to keep a close eye on Lily," Hezekiah said, nodding toward Lily as she sat at one of the wedding tables.

"Why?" She knew it too, but wondered if her husband thought the same as she.

"You know how she is. She thinks she has all the answers. She's impulsive and not completely trustworthy. I'm not saying that to be cruel, I'm only saying it out of concern for her. Lily doesn't care what we think and she doesn't listen to the cautions we give her."

"You're not telling me anything I don't know already," Nancy said.

"Are you still worried about her attraction to Nathanial Schumacher?"

Nancy looked over at Nathanial, who was one of the three boys jostling to talk to Lily. Lily only seemed to have ears for whatever Elijah Bontrager said.

"*Nee*, I'm not worried about him. She seems to have turned her attention in another direction."

"*Jah*, I can see exactly who you mean."

Nancy giggled. "But then again, I've always liked Matthew Schumacher."

"Me too."

"It's odd how cousins can be so different." Nancy took a sip of ginger beer.

"I know. I don't think you can judge people by their families sometimes. I know you think you can, but people can be born with their personalities set in stone. I've seen it before."

Nancy nodded. Since her husband was the deacon, many people came to him with their problems, and he was often at the bishop's house sorting out personal issues between people.

With her outgoing attitude where men were concerned, Lily had attracted more male attention than Daisy and her other two sisters. Nancy would be happy if Lily were to marry either Elijah Bontrager or Matthew Schumacher. Elijah was just slightly ahead of Matthew at the moment in the race for Lily's affections, in Nancy's opinion.

Lily and Elijah had become close in circumstances that had been entirely coincidental. Lily and Daisy were having the first fight they'd had and an accident involving a metal bucket and one of the windows in the front of the house had given Elijah cause to visit. Nancy was certain she'd never heard the true story of how the window came to be broken. Elijah was Ed Bontrager's oldest son and they were the local Amish glaziers. Ed had sent Elijah out to measure up the window to replace the glass.

Since then, Nancy had encouraged their relationship by often having Ed Bontrager and his boys over for dinner. Ed had been a widower for quite some time and the boys welcomed a chance to sample someone else's cooking. Ed had told Nancy that now the boys were teenagers they took it in turns to cook the meals at home.

Lily was the one doing all the talking, Nancy noticed, as she glanced back over at Lily and Elijah. As she studied Elijah's face, she noticed light and excitement in his eyes as he smiled and chatted with Lily. It was the youthful anticipation that young people had when they were convinced that they had life and the world all figured out. He had an enthusiastic glow of exuberance; the hard knocks of life hadn't yet had a chance to dull his confidence.

Nancy left her husband and hurried back to the

kitchen to check on what the ladies were up to with the food. The second sitting of the meal was about to take place. The day had been unseasonably cold and they had cleared and cleaned the barn just in case the weather changed and they had to have it under cover.

Lily still wasn't used to the idea that she'd lost her twin. If only Daisy had been patient they would've found and married twins like they'd always said. That idea had gone out the window as soon as Daisy had met Bruno. Daisy had cast that idea aside just as easily as one would discard a peel from a piece of fruit.

Lily would've thought she'd be more important than a man, but Daisy had made her choice and now she'd be gone for months. Lily had a suspicion that Bruno would persuade Daisy to live in Ohio. He hadn't sold his business like he'd told Daisy he would to help pay off the small home they'd purchased.

After Lily had expressed her concerns to Daisy, Daisy had stopped talking about their plans with Lily. In the past months, they'd grown apart. Daisy had drifted away and it was all because of Bruno. Lily had never even imagined that a man could come between them.

Lily knew she could get married as soon as she wanted. There were a few men who were interested in her and it would only take a small amount of encouragement before one of them would ask her to marry them, but there was no point in getting married in a hurried and mindless way. The way Daisy had been acting in the past months had put Lily off the idea of marriage all together. With marriage would come giving up part of herself and Lily was not willing to do that. In the past, Daisy would've never gone anywhere else to live, but now Lily was certain it wouldn't take much for Bruno to convince Daisy to live in Ohio, far away from her family.

Mrs. Walker, who owned a wholesale flower business, had previously offered Lily the opportunity to take over the job of selling flowers at the markets from Lily's sister, Rose. Right there at the wedding Lily found Mrs. Walker and finally accepted the job. Mrs. Walker was pleased and wanted her to start the very next day and Lily agreed. *The sooner, the better.*

The extra money and responsibility would give Lily a sense of empowerment that she'd never before experienced. And she was pleased about getting away from her mother and her two cousins.

Lily wondered whether marriage was really the answer for a happy life. She'd grown up to think that it was a milestone to be reached. Grow up, get married, have babies, have grandchildren—but was that all life was? There had to be more to life than to marry, have children, and then wait to die.

*I'm going to have a different life. One that is not boring!* Lily decided.

## Chapter Two

It had been a long boring night of cleaning up after the wedding. Lily slipped upstairs to bed before the others since she had to get up for her new job early the next morning.

She'd already carried out her plan for the marital bed and laughed to herself about it before she closed her eyes. Her job was a perfect excuse to get away from the house early that morning.

*Will Daisy and Bruno mention it to anyone?* she wondered.

Hopefully, they'd remain quiet about it and by the time Lily came home from work the next day, Daisy and Bruno would be long gone on their journey to Ohio, having not mentioned anything to anyone.

Just as she was drifting off to sleep, she heard her bedroom door open. She opened one eye slightly to see the silhouette of someone coming into her room. It was a small slender woman and had to be Daisy because the cousins were shorter and chubby. Lily froze. Daisy had found out about the short-sheeted bed and the sugar. Lily pretended to be asleep so Daisy couldn't get mad at her.

Daisy leaned over and shook her shoulder.

Lily pretended to wake up. She looked at Daisy, who was still in her mid-blue wedding dress, white cape, and white organza prayer *kapp*. "You gave me a fright."

"Sorry to wake you, but you didn't say goodbye to me or Bruno."

*Phew, she hasn't been to bed yet*, she thought. "You'll be coming back here, won't you?"

"*Jah*, we will, but not for a few weeks."

"Goodbye, and tell Bruno goodbye as well."

Daisy let out a sigh. "Why are you being like this?"

"Like what? You came here and woke me up and you know I've gotta get up early for work tomorrow. If you care to know what's happening in my life, I've just accepted the offer to work at the flower stall—Rose's old job."

"That's great."

"*Jah*, it is."

"You've been weird to me for weeks. Are you jealous of Bruno?"

Lily snorted. "*Jah*, that's right. I'm jealous of Bruno. Is that all? Can I go back to sleep now?"

"Why don't you say what's troubling you, Lily?"

"The only thing troubling me is you. I want to go to sleep and you're stopping me from doing that. Now, if you'll excuse me, I'll try to get back to sleep—if I can." Lily turned away from Daisy and put her head back on the pillow with her back now facing Daisy.

"Goodbye, Lily. I'll miss you."

"Please close the door on your way out." Lily lay quiet and still until she heard the door close. She hadn't meant to be rude to Daisy and she wouldn't have been if Daisy had just left her alone.

Lily got up extra early the next morning to avoid everyone. Her mother woke just as she was leaving the house.

With her hand on the front door handle, she heard her mother's voice behind her. "Lily, are you leaving for work already?"

Lily swung around. "I am. I've got a busy day ahead."

"It's too early. The market won't be open yet."

"I'm having breakfast out before I start." Lily reached for her black cape at the front door and slung it around her shoulders.

"Don't you want to stay and see Bruno and

*Amish Lily*

Daisy off? They've got an early start. You could say goodbye to them and still get to work on time."

Lily shook her head. "I said goodbye to them last night. Don't worry so, *Mamm*. It's all good." Lily smiled brightly, hoping her mother wouldn't make a fuss.

"Okay."

Once her mother nodded, Lily headed out the front door to hitch the horse to the buggy. The morning was bitterly cold, and the buggy her father allowed her to take had no heating system like some of the others had.

As her buggy clip-clopped along the roads toward town, Lily was wrapped in two blankets to keep out the cold. That morning, she'd put on two under-vests and two pairs of extra thick black tights. Her dress was of a heavier fabric much warmer than her summer ones.

Nancy didn't like to see Lily leave so early without bothering to say goodbye to Daisy. Daisy and Bruno were leaving in a taxi at eight to head to the local train station to begin their trip back to Bruno's home in Ohio.

After Lily had left, Nancy made breakfast for her husband and then waved him off. As soon as Nancy closed the door, she saw Daisy heading down the stairs.

"Morning, *Mamm*. Have I missed Lily?"

"*Jah*, she left very early, before your *vadder*."

"*Dat's* gone too?"

"You only just missed him, and Lily went a little before that."

"That's too bad. We said goodbye last night but I was hoping to catch her and *Dat* before they both left."

"Lily's a little upset that you're heading off so soon, I'd say. She didn't seem her normal self and she didn't need to leave as early as she did."

"I knew she'd be upset about me going to Ohio, but I told her we won't be gone for long."

"It's not just that. You two aren't as close as you once were."

Daisy followed her mother into the kitchen. "I know that. What can I do about it? I can't spend a lot of time with Bruno and her too. I can't split myself into two."

"I don't know what you can do. Just show her more attention when you get back, okay?"

"I will." Daisy giggled.

Her mother looked across at her. "What's so funny?"

"Last night, Bruno and I got into bed and someone had short-sheeted it."

"They what?"

"You know, folded the sheets over, so when we tried to get under the sheet our legs got caught in the fold."

"Oh. Who would've done that?"

Daisy put her fingertips to her mouth and giggled again. "Do you seriously have to ask?"

"Oh, Lily?"

"*Jah*. Then we found someone had put something grainy in the bed. Bruno said it was sugar."

Nancy's jaw dropped open. "That's dreadful. Poor Bruno."

"Don't worry. Bruno thought it was funny and so did I. I'll miss Lily so much and all the fun we used to have."

"I don't think it's funny at all. It's not a proper thing for a young lady to do. It just goes to show that she hasn't grown up yet." Nancy shook her head, and continued, "Well, no wonder she left so early this morning if she'd pulled that stunt."

Daisy stared straight ahead. "I'll write to her."

"You won't be gone that long, will you?"

"After I meet all Bruno's family, he wants to do some traveling so I can meet most of his other relatives."

Nancy pulled a face. "How long do you think you'll be gone?"

Daisy shrugged her shoulders. "I'm not certain."

"When you come back, you're staying on, aren't you?"

"*Jah*, I don't want to move away."

"Good."

Daisy smiled. "Bruno said when he sells his

business, he'll have enough money to pay a lot off our loan."

Nancy nodded, glad that Bruno had already told her husband and herself that, but words were fine—it was actions that counted. They had bought a house that Hezekiah had told them about. It was a reasonably priced house that was for sale close to Nerida's, but just because they bought a house didn't mean they were staying. Lily had often expressed her fears about Bruno keeping Daisy in Ohio, and Nancy hoped Lily wasn't right.

## Chapter Three

After having breakfast in the only diner she could find open at that early hour, Lily arrived to work just as one of the Walker boys was delivering the flowers to the stall. After she'd arranged the flowers, Matthew Schumacher turned up. Matthew had the stall next to hers where he sold his family's goat products—mostly cheese and yoghurt.

"Good morning, Lily," he said in his usual cheery manner. "I heard last night that you were starting here today. And a good thing too. Mrs. Walker was wearing herself out here at the stall and with all the work she had to do with running the business."

"Morning, Matthew." Matthew had always been a good friend and he'd grown up in the past two years into a man who was tall and reasonably attractive.

"That was a good wedding yesterday." While he spoke, he unloaded his trolley of products into the refrigerated displays.

"It was okay, I guess, as far as weddings go."

Matthew chuckled and glanced across at Lily. "How could it have been better?"

"I don't know." Lily really felt like saying it would've been better if her sister hadn't gotten married at all or had not gotten married to someone who could take her far away. They should've married twins just like they'd always said they would. But if she said that, Matthew might think she was crazy.

"Are you in one of your bad moods this morning, Lily?"

She swung around and stared at him, narrowing her eyes. "What do you mean?"

He laughed again. "See, that there. That's what I mean."

She shrugged her shoulders. "I don't see why people have to be happy all the time; there's no rule about that, is there? Anyway, everyone would get angry if you accused them of being so."

"To answer your question, I guess there's no rule about being angry or happy. It's more enjoyable to be around people who are cheerful. If you're grumpy all the time, you'll find that no one wants to be around you. I don't mean 'you'—I'm talking about people in general."

"Well, you don't have to talk to me, Matthew Schumacher. No one is forcing you."

Matthew placed the goods that were in his hands down and took a few steps closer to her. "Lily, I'm just trying to be your friend. If something's upsetting you, you can tell me what it is."

She saw the genuine concern on his face and was glad for the opportunity of someone to talk to. "I'm sorry, Matthew. You've always been nice to me. I'm just upset that Daisy is gone now and things will never be the same between us. We've always been together and done everything together. I've never been alone like this and it's ever since Bruno's come along."

Matthew nodded. "I can see how that would make you feel."

Lily's eyes widened. "You don't think I'm crazy?"

"Sometimes I do, but not about this. You must feel like you've lost part of yourself."

"I do, that's exactly how I feel. It's almost as though I don't know who I am anymore."

"You're the same person you always were, Lily. You're just the same."

"I don't know. I feel all jumbled up. We used to talk about everything and before I could figure out what I thought about a thing I'd talk to Daisy about it. Now she's gone. How will I know my opinions on everything without her?"

"It'll take some time to adjust to being without

Daisy living in your home. Where is she going to live, anyway?"

"Well, that's just it. I think that Bruno is secretly hoping that she'll stay in Ohio once they get there."

"Wouldn't they have talked about that before they got married?"

"I think Daisy will just go along with whatever he wants. She's lost her own mind and is just agreeing to whatever he says." Lily pushed out her lips as an image of Daisy's face smiling at Bruno came into her mind.

"Is there anything I can do to make you feel better?"

Lily shook her head. "I don't think so, but *denke* for asking."

"I better continue setting up."

Lily was pleased to have a friend in Matthew. He seemed to understand what she was going through. His older brother, Mark, was married to Lily's sister Rose and Matthew was often in attendance at the weekly family get-togethers that took place in Lily's home. He would've seen for himself how close she'd been with Daisy. Now Daisy had just walked away without a care in the world or a second thought for her.

Throughout the day, whenever Lily didn't have customers, she spent her time either chatting with Matthew or rearranging the flowers. She was in the middle of arranging some pink roses when a male voice scared her.

"How much for these?"

She jumped and turned around to see Elijah.

"What are you doing here?"

"I just finished one job and I'm on my way to another."

"And I thought you'd come to buy some flowers," she said.

"If that's what it takes to see you, then yes."

She turned and her eyes swept across the colorful variety of flowers. "Which ones take your fancy?" Lily's flirting with Elijah over the past several weeks was finally starting to pay off.

"It depends," he said.

She turned around to look into his eyes. "Depends on what?"

He rested his hands on his hips and grinned. "It depends on which ones *you* like."

Lily giggled. "Are they for me, or are you going to buy them for someone else and you want my opinion?"

"They're for you. Who else would I buy flowers for?"

Before she could answer, he took a step toward her and picked up cream roses with pink edges. "I know nothing about flowers, but these are quite beautiful. I didn't think roses would grow at this time of year."

"The Walkers grow the flowers in hot houses and whatever is out of season, they have flown in."

"That sounds expensive."

"Not really. They deal with other wholesalers. They're in some kind of co-op."

He looked down at the flowers. "Do you like them?"

"I like the yellow ones better." Lily had always been partial to yellow roses. She didn't really know why.

"I'll take a dozen of the yellow roses." He took a roll of paper money out of his pocket and peeled off some notes. "Keep the change."

"Are you sure? They don't come to anywhere near that."

"*Jah*. Take the flowers home and every time you look at them think about me. Will you do that?"

Lily stuffed the notes into the coin bag she kept buckled safely around her waist. "*Jah*, I will."

"Are you going to the ice-skating tonight?"

"I wasn't going to. But I've got my cousins staying and they'll probably want to go."

"Good. I'll see you there tonight." He glanced over at Matthew at the next stall, and then said quietly, "If you're going, I'll be there."

Lily watched him stride away. She liked everything about Elijah Bontrager. He was a no-nonsense, decisive person who always seemed in control. He might be the man she would marry if she ever decided to.

Matthew stood at the edge of his stall and called out, "What did *he* want?"

"He just bought me some flowers." She pointed to the yellow roses and wished she could stop smiling since she knew that Matthew liked her too and didn't want to hurt his feelings.

"Is that all it takes?"

"What do you mean?"

"Is that all it takes to put a smile on your face?" Matthew asked.

Lily grimaced. She didn't like being so easy to read, but she had to laugh. "I guess so."

"Humph. He didn't even say hello to me," Matthew grumbled.

Lily picked up her bunch of roses, walked over to Matthew and placed her thumb and forefinger just under one rosebud where the stem began. When she had pulled the flower from the bunch, she handed it to Matthew. "See, that made you smile. It works for you too. Everyone's happy when they're given flowers."

When Lily got home later that day, she walked into the kitchen, placed her roses in a vase and set them in the center of the table.

"They're lovely, Lily," her mother said, turning away from the stove.

"Someone gave them to me. That's why I brought them home."

"Who gave them to you?" Her mother rushed over to her and put a hand on her shoulder.

"Elijah."

"Elijah Bontrager?"

"*Jah.* Have Daisy and Bruno left yet?"

"They left early this morning. I told you that. You said goodbye to them, didn't you?"

"Of course I did."

"Your cousins tell me there's ice-skating on tonight and your *vadder* is hoping you'll take them there."

"Okay, that sounds good."

Her mother frowned at her. "Are you sure you don't mind?"

"I don't mind at all. I don't like ice-skating. I like watching it more than doing it."

"They say it's going to be a bit warmer tonight and there won't be that chill in the air like there has been over the last few days."

"That's good to know."

"You'll have to stop by Nerida's *haus* and pick up their skates. I've got some food packed for you to leave with Nerida."

"Okay." Not seeing the cousins anywhere about, she walked up to her mother and whispered, "Why can't they stay at their own place? They're old enough to look after themselves by now."

"I offered for them to stay and that's why they're here. That's what Nerida wanted too. She might have suggested it, but either way, it's a chance for Nerida to recover in peace and it might help Nerida and I to get back to where we once were."

"Aren't you friends with her now? You don't have to be like a slave to her looking after her *kinner*."

"Hush, Lily, it's not like that. It's not like that at all. I like doing things to help people."

That part was true. Lily knew her mother liked doing things for people and that's where Lily was different from the rest of her family. Her mother was always taking time to cook meals for the sick and the needy. In her spare time, when she wasn't visiting people, she was sewing or knitting things to sell for charity. It seemed to Lily that too many people in her family were too busy looking after other people while neglecting themselves. Her sisters were all doing what their husbands wanted and that was why she was sure Daisy was going to end up living in Ohio. She and Daisy would be apart forever. Daisy wouldn't even give her a second thought now she had Bruno—he had replaced her.

## Chapter Four

Lily set off to the ice-skating with her cousins right after they'd had the evening meal. While the horse clipped-clopped down the road, she thought about Elijah. Maybe the idea of marriage wasn't too bad. If she got married, she could have her own house and garden and have everything exactly how she wanted. She'd be out from under the control of her parents who watched her like hawks and judged every little thing she did. Matthew was nice, but he was more like a brother whereas Elijah would make a better boyfriend and husband. He'd also be a good provider and eventually he'd take over his father's business, seeing that he was the eldest son.

"Where are you going, Lily?"

She glanced over at Willow, her annoying

younger cousin. "Ice-skating. Isn't that where you want to go?"

"You missed the turn to *Mamm's haus*. We've got to get our skates, remember?"

"*Ach*, sorry." Lily turned the buggy around. She'd been so busy daydreaming about men she'd entirely forgotten she had to call in to her Aunt Nerida's house.

The cousins giggled at her forgetfulness. Lily smiled too at the sound of laughter because it reminded her of the good times that she and Daisy had when they got themselves into one lot of mischief after another.

When she stopped the buggy outside, the cousins jumped out while she took out the basket of food that her mother had packed for Nerida and John.

Uncle John met her outside the house. He had a long gray beard and his suspenders stretched tight over his large stomach. She'd never gotten along very well with him; he'd always looked at her suspiciously as though she was up to no good.

"Hello, *Onkel* John. How's Nerida?"

"Aunt Nerida is getting better."

Of course, he objected to her dropping the word 'aunt' from Nerida's name, but Lily figured herself old enough to call her Nerida. "Here." She handed him the basket of goodies. "This is from *Mamm*."

His face lit up. "Ah, thank her for us."

"I will. The girls are just getting their skates."

"*Jah*, I know," he said and then stared at her as though he was waiting for her to confess something she'd done.

"How much longer will her leg take to heal?" Lily asked to stop herself from wondering what he'd heard about her. He had to have heard something the way he was staring at her meanly.

He shook his head. "She shouldn't have been up on the roof. She should've left that to me. It was a nasty break."

"It sounds painful."

"She broke her femur. That's the main bone in the upper leg. They had to nail it together. They called it a 'metal rod,' but it works the same as a nail would."

Lily held her stomach, not wanting to hear any more details about nailing bones together. It sounded worse than any other broken bone she'd heard of—the ones that get set in plaster and bandages.

John didn't take the hint to stop giving the grisly information. "Then they had to screw the metal to the bone on either end."

"Oooh. Don't tell me any more."

"It was quite interesting. The doctor explained it all to me. Do you want to see the x-rays? You'll be able to see how it's broken and there's another one showing how they've fixed it."

Lily shook her head. "I certainly don't!"

He laughed. "Bit squeamish?"

"I never thought so."

"The doctor said it'd take between four to six months to heal properly."

Lily gasped. Did that mean the cousins would be staying at the house for that long? "That's a long time!"

*"Jah."*

"Who looks after Nerida during the day?"

"She's got two friends who take it in turns cooking and cleaning and generally looking after her."

"Who are they?"

"Shirley and Connie."

Lily nodded. "Ah. That's good of them."

"And your *mudder's* been so good to look after the girls. We know they're in good hands with you and your parents."

"Yeah, I'll look after them." Lily felt a little bad for being mean and bossy to them at times. "Can I see Nerida?"

"Aunt Nerida is resting now."

*Again with the 'aunt' business. What's his problem?* "Okay. Some other time, then."

*"Jah.* Why don't you come back through the day tomorrow?"

"I work six days a week. Well, five and a half really."

"That's right. You're working for the Walkers

now. You've taken over Rose's old job." He rubbed his beard. "Nerida mentioned that to me."

Lily nodded, amazed that Nerida had already heard. Then her cousins came running out of the house with their skates.

"Bye, *Dat*," the cousins both called out as they ran past their father to the buggy.

"Looks like we're off," Lily said, backing away from her uncle. "Say hello to Nerida for me and I'll come and visit when I can." She was pleased to get away before he could correct her to saying 'Aunt Nerida.' She had the last word and that's how she liked it.

"Did you see your *mudder*?" Lily asked the cousins when they were back on the road.

"She was sleeping."

"It sounds like she broke her leg really badly."

"*Jah*, we know. That's why we're staying with you."

"I didn't realize how bad."

"That's because you don't listen to anyone, Lily. You're too—" Willow gasped and it sounded to Lily as though Violet had dug her in the ribs.

"What am I too? Too what?" Lily pulled the buggy over to the side of the road and stopped. She stared at the cousins who appeared frightened. On seeing their fearful looks, she clicked the horse onward, not wanting to become someone who the cousins feared. "You two are too young to know anything much, so I'll ignore whatever you say or think."

"It was very kind of you to drive us tonight, Lily," Violet said in a small voice.

Willow added, "*Jah*, very kind, Lily."

## Chapter Five

Lily remained silent for the rest of the drive. Tonight they were skating at the huge frozen-over pond on the Millers' farm. When Lily pulled alongside the other buggies, Violet and Willow jumped out before she stopped.

They ran off, yelling a thank you to her over their shoulders.

It reminded Lily of how she and Daisy had always jumped out of the buggy when they were eager to get to a place, but possibly the cousins only did that to get away from her.

When the horse was secured, Lily pulled her shawl further around her shoulders to shield her from the cold night air. The cousins had wasted no time pulling on their skates. They were off skating on the ice as though that was where they belonged. Lily and her sisters hadn't skated often and as much fun as it looked, Lily knew she'd only spend most of the time on her bottom. She was too old to be embarrassed in that way.

There were five wooden benches arranged so people could either watch or rest from skating. Lily sat by herself, still not in the mood to talk with anyone, unless it was Elijah. She looked around and couldn't see him anywhere and told herself she might have been early and he'd arrive later. If he hadn't said he'd be there, she doubted she would've come at all, unless the cousins had persuaded her. Now she thought about it more, she could've traded some chores to drive the twins here. She was chuckling in her head when she sensed someone walking up beside her. It was Nathanial Schumacher.

"Mind if I sit?" he asked.

"It's not my seat." She looked down at the space next to her.

He sat down and placed a pair of skates at his feet. "It was a good wedding yesterday."

"I guess."

"I heard your *schweschder* is moving to Ohio."

"*Nee*, she's not. Where did you hear that?"

His eyes widened. "I don't remember."

"She's not moving there. She's simply going there to meet all her new relations."

"Maybe she won't come back," he said, leaning closer.

"Are you trying to upset me?"

"*Nee*, I wouldn't be brave enough to do that. I'm sorry, I didn't know it was such a sore subject."

Lily scowled at him. "Are you a twin?"

He chuckled. "Not unless my *mudder* kept a secret from me. She could've given my twin away." He laughed as though he'd said something funny. "*Nee*, I've never had a twin."

"It's not something to joke about. Unless you've been a twin you wouldn't understand."

"I've never asked you, but I've always wondered. What is it like being a twin?"

"Being a twin is like being a twin." She stared at his confused face, and explained, "How would I know? I've never been anything else."

"Well, what do you think the best thing is about being a twin?"

"Being a twin."

He rubbed his forehead. "Can you explain it?"

"I'll try. It's always having her there. We never had to talk about things. There were things we just knew. And we thought the same about everything."

"I'll miss her too. I liked her."

"*Jah*, well, she didn't like you enough, did she?"

"Ouch! You've got quite a sting in your words tonight."

Lily turned away from him and stared at the skaters as they glided freely on the ice. If only she could skate like that, she'd feel free. It was too late to learn now.

He leaned closer. "What you need is some cheering up."

"And you're the person to help me do that?"

"Exactly."

"What did you have in mind? Are we going to try drugs, perhaps knock over a supermarket? Maybe we'll steal a car."

"Oh, so sarcastic, and now you leave me with no original suggestions."

She looked around, hoping Elijah might save her from Nathanial, but he was still nowhere to be seen. Perhaps he'd changed his mind about coming.

"Well, what did you have in mind?" she asked him.

"Nothing quite as daredevil as you mentioned."

"That's just as well because we might have landed in jail. The bishop wouldn't be impressed either."

"Neither would your parents."

They both laughed. It had been a while since she'd laughed and it felt good.

Nathanial said, "Why don't I take you out for dinner somewhere next week?"

"I don't—"

"I'll take you anywhere you want. It doesn't have to be dinner. Come on, Lily, I'm going crazy here away from my friends. I don't know many people here, you know that."

"If you want friends, all you have to do is be more friendly."

"*Jah*, well, your *schweschder* kind of ruined my chances of people around here ever trusting me."

Lily nodded, thinking back to a long time ago when Daisy had said that Nathanial attacked her. They'd both had different sides to their stories and as much as Lily loved Daisy, she knew she was prone to exaggeration and craved attention. "Daisy only cares about herself sometimes."

"Forget about her. Come on, what do you say? Will you save me from one night of boredom next week?"

Weakening and wanting to feel better, she asked, "What night?"

She took another look around and saw Elijah's buggy. He had just pulled up next to her buggy.

"How about Tuesday?" he asked.

"*Nee*, I'm sorry. I can't."

"What night, then?"

"No night would be suitable."

"Come on, Lily. You're the only girl around here who understands me."

She shook her head. "Like I said, try being friendly with people and then you'll have more friends."

He swept his eyes over the skaters and the people watching. "It's not that. No one is suitable."

She laughed at him feeling sorry for himself and then swiveled in her seat. When she looked up, she noticed Elijah walking toward her and she waved to him.

"I won't give up," Nathanial said when he saw Elijah.

Elijah greeted both of them and then sat on the other side of Lily. Soon after Elijah sat down, Nathanial grabbed his skates.

"I'll see you both later. I'm going to watch the skaters."

"Okay." Lily noticed Nathanial had his skates with him whereas Elijah had nothing in his hands, which most likely meant that he'd only come to speak with her.

"How are things?" Elijah asked when they were alone.

"About the same as they've been for the past few days."

"Missing Daisy?"

"I'm trying not to think about her, but it's a hard thing to do. Everything reminds me of her. Every place I go and everything I do reminds me of her."

"Sorry, I won't mention her again."

Lily gave a laugh. "It's okay."

"Was Nathanial bothering you? He took off pretty quickly when I sat down."

"*Nee*, he's all right." Lily assumed he must've heard some of the talk and rumors that surrounded Nathanial. It seemed no one trusted him and she often wondered what the truth of the matter had been. Maybe she'd never know. Her father said there were two sides to every story.

"I hope so," Elijah said.

"*Denke* again for the flowers. They're on the kitchen table at home and they look beautiful."

"I'm glad you like them. I wasn't sure you would after being around flowers all day."

"I do, I love them."

"I'll remember that. Lily, I wanted you to come here tonight because I want to—"

An ear-splitting squeal carved through the night air. Lily whipped her head around toward the ice to see that three people had collided and one of those people was Willow.

"Willow!"

## Chapter Six

Lily jumped up and ran toward her, while slipping and sliding across the ice with Elijah right behind her. Nathanial had reached Willow first and was helping her to her feet.

"Are you okay?" Nathanial asked her.

When Lily got there, she elbowed Nathanial out of her way.

"I'm okay," Willow said while trying not to cry.

Now Violet had skated to them and was also by her side. "Are you all right, Willow?"

Willow rubbed her arm and cringed. "*Jah*, I think so, but my shoulder hurts."

Lily looked around at the other two people who didn't appear to have suffered any injuries and had picked themselves up.

"Maybe we should take her to the hospital to get checked out," Elijah suggested.

"*Nee*, I'm fine. Please don't make a fuss. I don't like hospitals. I just want to go home. I'm okay."

She hung her head after she'd taken a look around at everyone gathered around her. Lily guessed she was embarrassed. "Of course, we'll go home. Come on, Violet, let's go."

Violet put her arm around Willow's waist as they made their way to the bench so they could take off their skates.

Lily turned to look at Nathanial and Elijah. "*Denke* for being there, both of you."

"As long as she's okay," Nathanial said.

"She seems to be. She might be sore for a couple of days, but that's it. That's what I'm guessing," Lily said.

Lily left Nathanial to skate some more while she and Elijah walked over to the girls. The girls put their boots on while Elijah collected their skates.

"I'll help you to the buggy," Elijah said.

Nancy was drifting off to sleep when she heard the buggy arrive home. Hearing them finally home gave her a sense of peace and she drifted off to sleep. She was jolted awake when she heard Lily yelling from downstairs.

"*Mamm*, come quick."

Something about the tone in Lily's voice jagged at the pit of Nancy's stomach.

Hezekiah raised his head. "What is it? What—"

"Go back to sleep. You know how Lily can be. It's probably nothing."

Hezekiah put his head back on the pillow while Nancy whipped a robe on and rushed downstairs. As soon as she was at the foot of the stairs, she looked up to see that the other two girls had their arms around Willow. She rushed toward them. "Willow, what's wrong?"

"It's nothing. I just fell over and my shoulder's a bit sore."

"She collided with two other people and fell heavily on the ice," Lily explained.

"Let me see." Nancy pressed around Willow's shoulder to see what parts were tender. "It doesn't appear that you've broken anything, but I think you'll be very sore in the morning. What you need is a good hot bath with lots of salts."

"That sounds good," Willow said with a small smile.

"Lily, you go fill the bath while I find another hot water bottle for her for tonight. I know I've got a spare one somewhere."

The two girls walked with Willow to the bathroom.

"It's one thing after another," Nancy mumbled to herself before she yelled out to the girls again. "I'll fix you all some hot chocolate." She didn't hear any reply, but she knew the girls would like hot chocolate with marshmallows. After she had lit the stove, she placed the pot on to boil. To warm herself, she stood as close as she could to the stove without getting burned.

She'd thought nothing of getting out of the warm bed when she'd heard Lily. In spite of what she told her husband, she'd known that something was wrong. Even though Nerida and she hadn't been close in the past few years, Nerida's children were still like her own. The bond of family was a strong one.

Nancy wondered whether it was Lily's fault that Willow had fallen. There was always drama whenever Lily was around, but perhaps this time it was just a genuine accident. Half convinced that all Willow needed was a hot bath tonight and to keep her shoulder warm until morning, she realized a trip to the doctor might be necessary if it wasn't better the following day.

"That's the phone." Lily ran outside to the barn and grabbed the phone before the person hung up. It took so long to get to the barn that they often missed calls altogether.

"Who have I got?" the person on the other end asked.

"It's Lily. Is this Mark?"

"It is. Can you tell your *mudder* it's time?"

"Time for what?"

"We're having a *boppli*."

"*Nee!*"

"*Jah*, we are. Tell your *mudder* we need her."

"Right now?" Lily asked, worried about Willow.

"Rose needs your *mudder* now."

"I'll get her. Do you want to speak with her?"

"*Nee*, just tell her Rose is having contractions."

Lily shivered at the thought of all the pain her sister was about to go through. "She'll be there soon." Lily hung up without saying goodbye and ran into the house yelling. "*Mamm, Mamm!*" She found her mother in the kitchen looking quite annoyed with her.

"Why are you screaming for me? What's wrong now?"

"Rose is having the *boppli* now. Mark said she's having contractions."

Her mother gasped. "Has Mark called the midwife yet?"

"I don't know. Should I have asked that?"

A look of fear covered her mother's face. "*Nee, nee*, it's okay. I'll get ready." She turned around and switched the stove off.

"I'll call him back and ask him about the midwife."

"*Nee*, don't. It's all right. I'll have to gather some things and go right now. I don't know how far along she is or how long I'll be gone." She pressed her lips together and rubbed her forehead. "Can you look after Willow?"

"Of course I can. I'll get her a hot water bottle and see to it she's okay. I'll rub her shoulder with wintergreen oil."

"*Jah*, *gut* idea." Shaking her head, *Mamm* said, "It never rains but it pours. Things always seem to happen all at the same time."

"Just go, *Mamm*. He said Rose needs you and he said she was contracting and that sounds painful."

"Having contractions," her mother corrected.

"Either way, I'm glad it's not me going through it."

Violet walked into the kitchen. "What's happened?"

"Rose is in labor," Lily said.

"Oh."

"You'd better go, *Mamm*," Lily told her mother.

"*Jah*, I'm going." Nancy strode out of the kitchen.

Violet hurried after Nancy and then Hezekiah appeared at the foot of the stairs.

"It's Rose's time. Not only that, Willow came home with a bad shoulder from falling heavily on the ice," Nancy informed him.

"Do you want me to help you hitch the buggy, Aunt Nancy?" Violet asked.

Hezekiah said, "I can do that, Violet. You stay here and look after your *schweschder*."

## Chapter Seven

Hezekiah and Nancy went out to the barn and got the horse and buggy ready.

"I'll call as soon as the *boppli's* born."

"I won't hear the phone, not if I'm asleep," Hezekiah said.

"Lily will. If you're asleep, I'll have her wake you."

"Okay. How long do you think the *boppli* will take to be born?"

"I'm not sure. Mark gave absolutely no indication of how far along she is. Lily spoke to him on the phone."

"Are you sure you got the correct message, then?"

"I think so, from what she said. It sounds like Rose might be in the very early stages. I told him to call me at the first sign. It might take a whole day, or longer."

"I'll stop by their *haus* before work tomorrow if you're not home by then," he said.

"Very good."

"I hope all goes safely. I'll pray that the *boppli* is healthy and Rose comes through it and both will be well."

"Me too. I don't care whether it's a boy or a girl as long as the *boppli* is in good health. *Gott* willing."

"That's the main thing."

Once the horse was hitched to the buggy, Hezekiah held out his arms and Nancy stepped in for one of Hezekiah's large hugs. She was always comforted in his arms.

"Look after the girls, won't you?" she said.

"I'll do my best, but I think Lily's got everything under control."

Nancy laughed. "That would be a first, and that was something I never thought I'd ever hear you say."

Hezekiah chuckled. "Sometimes we don't know what people can do until they are faced with responsibility."

"I guess you're right. She is the youngest, and she's never had anybody else to look after. Now she has her two younger cousins."

"The responsibility hasn't hurt her at all. I think she's maturing."

Nancy stepped back "If you don't hear from me, I'll see you in the morning at Rose's place."

"*Gut nacht*, my dear."

"*Gut nacht.*" After giving her husband a quick kiss, Nancy left her family behind and trotted the buggy to Rose's house. She only wished Mark had given more information so she knew what she'd be faced with once she got there.

She knocked on the door and when no one answered, she opened it and walked in. "Hello?"

Mark walked out of the bedroom to greet her. "Nancy! Hello."

"How far along is she?" Nancy asked.

"Clara said she's got a long way to go yet. But she can't be that far away because Clara said she'd stay rather than come back later. Come and see her."

Nancy walked into the bedroom to see Rose walking around and Clara, the Amish midwife, sitting in a chair knitting. She nodded hello to Clara and was pleased Rose didn't look too stressed.

"Hi, *Mamm.* I'm glad you're here. I've got all the pain across my back at the moment. No pain at the front. Every contraction is kind of across my back."

Nancy looked at the midwife. "Is that normal?"

"Everything is progressing normally. I think we only have a few hours to go."

"Really? My first labor was quite long. Well, the first one was, the rest were relatively quick."

"Rose's already progressed far in the last few hours."

"Few hours?" She shot a look at Mark. She'd told him she wanted to be present from the very start to the finish.

He dipped his head. "I didn't want to bother you. We thought it might be one of those false alarms."

"Rose, I told you I wanted to be called. I wanted to be here with you the entire time."

"I thought it'd make me too anxious and I wasn't sure what it was when the pains started. I thought it might have been the flu."

Nancy couldn't say anything more because she didn't want her daughter to be stressed. "Can I do anything?"

"All we can do now is wait," the midwife said.

With her mother gone, Lily felt like she was in charge and she liked the way that made her feel. Now she was pleased that her cousins were there because it was more fun to be with girls while her mother was out of the house, rather than just be alone with her father. At least she could boss her cousins around. She figured she'd have that feeling of being in charge all the time when she became a mother.

Lily's father walked back into the house after her mother left to look after Rose. It was quite unbelievable that Rose was actually having a baby. She was the first of her sisters to do so.

"All we can do now is wait," Hezekiah said as he sat down on the couch with Lily.

"*Jah*, but for how long?"

"Only *Gott* knows the answer to that one. It could be a few hours or several."

For Rose's sake, Lily hoped it would only be a few.

Violet sat down on the couch with them.

"How's Willow?" Hezekiah asked.

"She's okay. She's in bed now keeping warm with a hot water bottle on her shoulder."

"I'll go up and see if she needs anything," said Lily.

"She's fine. I just left her. She just wants to sleep."

"Okay." Lily wanted to do something. She wanted to go and help Rose, but her mother had everything under control. "Does anybody want a cup of hot tea or a cup of hot chocolate? *Mamm* was starting to make some before she left."

"I wouldn't mind a mug of hot chocolate," her father said.

"*Jah*, me too please, Lily."

"Okay." Lily jumped to her feet, pleased to have something to do.

"I'll help," Violet said.

"*Nee*, I can do it."

In the early hours of the morning, Rose held her baby girl in her arms.

Nancy stood back, allowing Mark to have a private time with his wife and brand-new daughter. She proceeded to help the midwife clean up the room.

"Come and have another look at her, *Mamm*."

"Okay, I'll just wash my hands." After Nancy washed her hands carefully, she peered over and had another look in the baby's face. She was healthy and she was perfect. "You just forget how tiny they are at this young age."

"We're calling her Sarah."

"That's a beautiful name," Nancy said.

Mark said, "I'll call everyone. I've got a long list of people who asked to be called." He chuckled. "I can't wake everyone at this late hour of the night. I'll just call the closest family."

"Of course," Nancy commented as Mark walked out of the room to the phone they had in the barn.

Nancy hoped that the baby would soften Rose's heartache over the two miscarriages she'd had. She'd been devastated, but looking at her now, she'd never seen her daughter look so happy.

"I'll tell everyone to give you a couple of days before they visit you," Nancy said.

"What about *Dat*? When's he coming?"

"He'll come over first thing in the morning if that's all right."

"Of course it is."

Lily slept on the couch, so she would be closest to the phone in the barn. She wanted to be the first one to hear news of Rose's baby. She was certain Rose was having a boy and everybody else was certain she was having a girl. More than anything, Lily wanted to be right.

When she first heard the phone ringing, a ringing phone played out in the dream she was experiencing. Then she jolted herself awake, threw back the quilt, grabbed a flashlight and raced out the door. Just when she got to the phone in the barn, it stopped ringing. Immediately, she called Rose's number, figuring it must be Mark calling with news. Who else would it be at that time of night?

Mark picked up the phone immediately. "Hello?"

"Mark, has she had the *boppli*?"

"Who's this?"

"It's Lily."

"I was just calling you."

"I know. I just reached for the phone and it stopped. Quick, tell me the news!"

"Rose and I have a *dochder*."

"You do?"

*"Jah."* He chuckled.

"That's *wunderbaar* news. Congratulations. I'll wake everyone up. They'll all be very excited."

Mark chuckled again. "I've got a list of people to call."

"I won't hold you up. Is Rose okay?"

"Things went wonderfully well. The midwife said it was a fast birth for a first *boppli.* And she's healthy."

*"Gut. Denke* for letting us know, Mark."

"Bye, Lily." The receiver clicked in her ear.

Lily hung up and, with the flashlight illuminating her way, walked back to the house in the darkness. She raced back into the house as fast as she could. The first person to hear the news should be her father. It was still dark, so she flashed her light onto the clock on the mantle to see what time of the morning it was. After she ran up the stairs two at a time, she ran into his room. *"Dat!"*

He sat bolt upright. "What?"

"The *boppli's* here. Rose's *boppli.*"

"Is Rose okay?"

"Mark said she's fine. She's only just been born."

"She?"

*"Jah*, she's a girl."

"Good." He rubbed his beard. "A girl. That is *gut* news. What time is it?"

She had to think hard with her brain being so foggy. "Two thirty."

"I'll stop by and see her before work. Will your *mudder* still be there, or is she coming home?"

"I don't know. No one said anything. She might stay the night there. I'm going to wake the cousins and tell them. *Gut nacht, Dat.*" Lily leaned over and kissed her father on his forehead before she hurried out of his room.

"*Gut nacht,* Lily."

It felt strange to Lily that one of her sisters had a *boppli* of her own. It was different when her sisters-in-law had babies. She couldn't wait to see Rose and the new baby, but she'd have to wait until after work.

She went into Violet's room and on hearing her snoring softly, didn't have the heart to wake her. Peeping into Willow's room, she saw her moving slowly and uncomfortably. "Psst, Willow."

Willow turned around, whimpered, then opened her eyes before she sat up. "What's going on?"

"I've got another niece."

"True? Rose's had the *boppli* already?"

"*Jah*, a girl."

"Oh, that's *wunderbaar*. Can we go see her now?"

"*Nee*, Rose will be tired," Lily said.

"Does Violet know?"

"*Nee*, she's snoring."

Willow giggled. "I'll tell her in the morning."

"Okay."

"Now I won't be able to sleep," Willow said.

"Me either, but I'm going to try my best. I have to work." Lily sighed. "Anyway, how are you feeling now? How's your shoulder?"

"Everything's aching. That's why I haven't slept. I can't get comfortable."

"Can I get you something? Give me the hot water bottle and I'll make it hot again."

"*Nee*, that's okay. It doesn't really help." Willow exhaled deeply. "I don't think so anyway. I just wish I could get some sleep."

"I'll see you in the morning. If you need anything, yell out. I don't think I'll be sleeping much either. I'm too excited."

"Okay, *denke*. Night, Lily."

*"Gut nacht."* Lily headed downstairs and then dragged her pillow and quilt back to the comfort of her own bed. Slipping between the covers, she thought about her sisters and how all of them had married good men. Would she remain the odd one out? Daisy had met Bruno quite unexpectedly. Rose and Mark had worked close together at the markets for years. And Tulip had met Wilhem through his cousin, Jonathon.

## Chapter Eight

When Lily got to work the next morning, she couldn't wait to tell Matthew about the baby.

"Guess what, Matthew?"

"I know. Your *schweschder* and Mark have a *dochder*."

"What? How did you hear that already?"

"Um… Mark is my *bruder*."

"That's right." Lily felt silly. Of course he would've heard about it. Mark would've called him.

Matthew added, "It's only normal he'd tell his family."

Lily laughed. "I'm quite dumb sometimes."

He smiled and shook his head. "You said it, not me."

Lily ignored his comment. Nothing would upset

her today. "I'm going to stop by tonight and see her."

"That's exciting for you. Tell Rose I said hi."

"I will. When are you going to see the *boppli*?"

"When I'm invited."

"Do you think that I should wait to be invited?"

"*Nee*. Your Rose's *schweschder*, so that's different."

"Oh, I didn't know that."

"Girls and *bopplis*...you know?"

"What? You mean men aren't interested in *bopplis*?" Lily asked.

"That's right—not especially. Unless they're their own."

"This is your niece, though, Matthew."

"Yeah, I know and I'll still wait until I'm invited."

Lily shook her head. "You're way too polite, Matthew."

"*Denke.*"

Lily pulled a face. "That's not a compliment."

"I know you didn't mean it as one, but I'm taking it as one."

"Men!" Lily got busy serving some customers and then when she became free again, she looked over at Matthew. A man had been talking to him for quite a while without buying anything. The man wore a dark suit and tie, which made him look kind of official and important.

When the visitor left, Lily walked over to Matthew's stall. "Did you know that man who was just here?"

"*Jah*, he's my distributor."

"Distributor for what?"

"For the products I've created."

Lily was intrigued and stepped closer. "What products?" This was the first time she was hearing about products. They'd talked so much yesterday in between customers, it was strange he hadn't mentioned products then.

"I've created a line of goats' milk skincare."

Lily burst out laughing. Skincare was the last thing she would think an Amish man would care about. When he just stood there looking rather hurt, she stopped laughing and cleared her throat. There was a small chance he was serious. She had guessed that since his family ran a goat dairy farm the products might have been to do with goats, but thought it would be something edible.

"For real?" she asked.

He nodded. "*Jah*, for real. I saw similar products out there and I thought why not get into that?"

Lily raised her eyebrows and placed her hand over her stomach, trying not to laugh. "Isn't skincare for women?"

"*Jah*, the products are for women."

Lily stared at him, trying not to laugh. He was

simply ridiculous and his face was so serious. "But you're a man."

"It doesn't matter. Men can create products for women. They don't have to be made by women."

His quiet confidence made her think twice. "How do you even know anything about skin-care?"

"Well, we've got goats—obviously—so I thought there's no reason that my family and I couldn't do more with our range other than just products people can eat. We're increasing our range."

"And what was, or what is, that man doing for you?"

"He's getting the products into pharmacies and department stores."

"Really? And your family's agreed to this?"

"I'm kind of doing it by myself. They don't want to take their focus off the dairy."

She stared at Matthew, seeing him in a new light. He was a real man, a man who got things done, and he would make some woman a wonder-ful provider.

"I'm impressed with what you've done, Mat-thew. This is a big thing."

His eyes opened wider. "Really?"

She nodded. "I'm sorry I laughed about it. I shouldn't have. It was foolish of me. It sounded strange. I guess it sounded strange because it was so unexpected. You've done something really *wunderbaar*! And you thought of this all on your own?"

"*Jah*, after I saw other goats' milk products, but I'm sure mine are better. I got together with a chemist to create the range. It's free of nasty chemicals."

"Wow!" Lily glanced over and saw customers approaching. "I'd like to hear more about it later."

"You would?"

"*Jah*." Lily giggled. "You might be able to give me some free samples."

Lily was pleased to have a job at last. It gave her some independence. Now she was on her way to see Rose and her baby on the way home from work. She hadn't needed to consult anyone about it. If she'd been at home all day, she would've needed permission to leave and to use the buggy.

When she reached the house, she was pleased that there were no buggies there.

She walked up to the door and knocked on it and within seconds Mark opened the door.

"Lily, come in."

"Is Rose awake?"

"*Jah*." He chuckled. "We haven't had much sleep."

"I can come back later if it's a bad time."

"*Nee*, come in. Rose would like to see you. Your *mudder* went home earlier."

"Did *Dat* come?" Lily asked as she walked through the front door.

"Early this morning." Mark led the way to the bedroom where Rose was lying in bed with her baby curled up beside her rather than in the crib.

Lily rushed forward and looked at the baby. "Oh, Rose, she's so tiny." Then she gave Rose a hug. "How does it feel to be a *mudder*?"

"It's better than anything. I love her more than anything already."

Lily glanced up at Mark to see how he took that news.

He chuckled. "It's okay, Lily. I'd already figured out where I stood."

Rose continued, "There's nothing like a *mudder's* love and now I know what it feels like. I loved her when she was inside me, but now she's out and…it's just more real. And now I can hold her."

"I'll leave you two alone." Mark backed away.

"Do you need anything, Rose? I should've thought to bring you something."

"I've got everything I need."

There was another knock on the door.

"Who could that be?" Rose asked.

Lily raced to the window. "It's *Mamm* with Violet."

"Oh, *gut*."

"Has Tulip already been to see you?"

"*Nee*."

"So, I've been the first *schweschder* to see Sarah?"

"*Jah.* You have."

Lily was delighted about that.

Soon, the other guests were shown into Rose's room.

They all waited anxiously for the baby to wake up so they could hold her. Rose didn't want anyone to disturb her while she was asleep. They sat on the edge of Rose's bed except for Violet who sat cross-legged on the rug on the floorboards.

"Where's Willow?" Rose asked.

"She had a hard fall when she was ice-skating and she didn't feel well enough to come," Violet said.

"I hope she'll be all right."

"She will. She just needs to rest," Nancy said.

When they heard another buggy, they all looked out the window.

"Who is it?" Rose asked.

"It's Tulip!" Violet said.

They all waited while Mark showed her into Rose's room. Tulip hugged Rose and then turned her attention to the small sleeping baby. "She's beautiful, so beautiful." Then Tulip cleared her throat. "There's something I want to tell everybody."

Everybody looked at Tulip expectantly and remained silent. "Sarah will soon have a cousin."

Nancy leaped to her feet. "You're not, are you?"

Tulip nodded and then her mother wrapped her arms around her. "That's the best news I've heard in a long time."

The other girls hugged Tulip and then congratulated her.

"I've got so many nieces, but only one nephew. You might have to fix that, Tulip," Lily said.

"Then it will be Daisy's turn," Violet said.

That wasn't what Lily wanted to hear. They were supposed to get married together and have babies together, she and Daisy. Now her twin would be way ahead of her.

"Not necessarily," Nancy answered, looking at Lily. "It could be some time off."

Lily knew her mother was only saying that because she knew how Lily felt deep down. "It's okay, *Mamm*. It's the truth. The days of Daisy and I doing everything together are over. She's gone, and she's out of my life completely."

Lily looked up when she felt Tulip glaring at her. "Can't something just be about me for once? Why do you constantly need the attention focused on you all the time? Daisy is just the same. Can't everyone be happy for once?"

"We are happy for you," Nancy said.

Tulip wiped tears out of her eyes. "I didn't tell anyone until after Daisy's wedding because I didn't want to take the attention away from her. That's why I waited until Rose's *boppli* was born too. When is it my turn to get some attention?"

"Your husband should give you attention," Lily said, feeling no sympathy for her at all. "Daisy got married and she doesn't want any attention from anyone else apart from her husband."

"I'm not as selfish as you, Lily," Tulip blurted out.

"I don't want any angry talk around my *boppli*," Rose said, frowning at her sisters. "This isn't how her first day in the world should be."

"You're right, Rose. It's not good for the *boppli*. If you two want to argue, do it outside somewhere," Nancy said, glaring at Tulip and then Lily.

"I'm sorry, Rose," Lily said.

Tulip nodded. "Me too."

"That's okay. I'm happy for you, Tulip. Our *bopplis* will be about the same age. How far along are you?" Rose asked.

"Around four months."

"Four months and you didn't say anything?" Nancy was clearly horrified.

"*Nee*, I didn't want to take attention away from Daisy's wedding, like I said."

Nancy shook her head. "It wouldn't have mattered."

"Four months. That means they'll be so close in age."

Lily stayed quiet while everyone talked about

Tulip being pregnant. Lily was pleased for her, but she didn't need to be so horrid. How could Tulip say that she wanted all the attention? Daisy was the one who'd gotten all the attention just recently because of the wedding.

Nancy could wait no longer for the baby to wake up. She picked her up carefully and cradled her in her arms. She placed her cheek against the baby's soft head. "She is so precious."

Violet touched her small arm. "She sure is."

"Can I have a hold?" Lily asked after a while.

"I was just about to ask," Tulip said.

"Okay, we'll go oldest down," Rose said. "Tulip next, then Lily, and then Violet."

When Lily's turn came, she held her carefully, and then the baby opened her eyes and looked up at her. "She's got her eyes open and she's staring at me."

"She's not crying," Violet said.

"Oh, she did last night. She's got a funny little cry. Mark and I were changing her diapers all night long. I don't know where all of it came from."

"Yuk," Violet said.

"Tell me about it," Rose said with a giggle.

"I'm going to make my husband change the diapers," Violet said.

"I hope you succeed," Nancy said. "They usually find some excuse to get out of it."

"Mark's been *gut* so far, but he's only got a

couple more days off work and then I'll be home alone."

"I can stop by after work to see if you need help," Lily said.

"I can come every day. It'll give me something to do," Tulip said. "And I can learn what to do a little better."

"Sounds good," Rose said.

Lily passed the baby to Violet.

"Mind her head," Nancy said.

"I know," Lily and Violet said at the same time, which made them laugh.

"I want one," Violet said.

"You'll want to wait until you get married," Lily said.

"I know that," Violet said. "I'm not in a hurry. I don't even like anyone yet, but as soon as I get married, I'll have one of these immediately."

"They seem a lot of work," Lily said. "As beautiful as they are. Waking up to changing stinky diapers doesn't sound like much fun."

"Everything is work according to you," Tulip said.

Lily didn't respond. She'd never seen Tulip so objectionable. Maybe it was the hormones affecting her brain.

"It's not work, Lily. It's just something you do out of love," Rose said.

"Yeah, well. I'll find out one day I suppose."

"Not if you don't get married," Nancy snapped.

Lily frowned at her mother. "I know that. I'm not silly. So, how was the birth? Was it dreadful?"

"It wasn't how I thought it would be. It wasn't too bad. I survived."

"Oh *gut*," Tulip said. "I'll ask you more about it later."

Violet's body shuddered. "I don't want to hear the details until I *have* to know."

"It's different for everyone," Nancy assured her.

Lily said, "I'll leave now and see how Willow is." She leaned over and gave Rose a kiss on the cheek. "Your *boppli* is beautiful."

"She is. I'm so thankful she's well and healthy."

"I'll stop by quickly after work tomorrow. Do you want me to bring you anything from the markets?" Lily asked.

"I can't think of anything, but you could ask Mark on your way out. We might be low on something."

"Okay."

Lily made her way to the front door and saw Mark sitting on the couch reading the newspaper.

"Leaving already?" he asked.

"*Jah*, Willow's at home because she had a nasty fall at ice-skating. I don't want to be away from home too long. Do you need anything from the markets? I'm stopping by after work tomorrow, just briefly."

"*Jah*, if you don't mind. That'll save me going out. We need a bag of potatoes and two loaves of bread, if you could."

"No problem."

"Wait there, I'll get you some money."

"Not necessary. I think I can afford a bag of potatoes and some bread."

"*Nee*, just wait and I'll get the money. It's just in the kitchen."

"I've got it covered. It's no problem."

He chuckled. "Are you certain?"

"Of course. I've got a job now."

He laughed again. "*Denke*. I heard you've taken over Rose's old job at the Walkers' flower stall. I hope you're keeping my *bruder* in line."

"I'm trying to. Your *boppli* is beautiful, Mark," she said as she walked to the front door.

He got there first and opened the door for her. "*Denke*, Lily."

## Chapter Nine

When Lily got home, she found Willow in the bathroom having a hot bath.

She said through the bathroom door, "A hot bath will do your back good."

"*Jah*, it feels better while I'm in the bath."

"I'll get something for us to eat while everyone is looking at the *boppli*. I don't think they'll be home for a while. And *Dat* is going there after work too."

"Why didn't you stay on? I would've been fine here on my own."

"It's not nice to be on your own and not feeling well."

"Did you come home specially to see me?" Willow asked.

"Well, that, and Tulip was being horrible to me."

Still in the bath, Willow called out, "Why's that?"

"Oh, you probably don't know. I only just found out myself. Tulip is having a *boppli*."

Willow squealed. "Really? When?"

"She said she's four months along."

"That means her *boppli* and Rose's will be born in different years, but still close in age."

"That's true."

"So why was she being horrible to you, Lily?"

"I'll talk to you when you get out of the bath. It's hurting my voice to yell."

"Okay. Fix me something nice to eat," Willow cheekily ordered.

Lily giggled at her cousin. "Okay. I'll see what I can find." When she walked into the kitchen, she smelled cooked food. To her delight, there was a huge dish of creamed celery and bacon keeping warm in the oven. "Ah, I like it when *Mamm* thinks ahead."

She took the bread out of the bread crock and sliced it thickly. Then she set the table for two. When Willow finally got out of the bath and dressed, she sat down at the kitchen table.

"How do you feel?"

"Better after the bath."

"Did you know that *Mamm* cooked this?"

Willow giggled. "I helped her."

"*Denke*. I can't wait to eat some. I suppose we should leave some for the others."

"Unfortunately, I suppose we should." Willow handed her plate across to Lily who filled her plate. "I won't be blamed for taking too much. I'll say you served me." Willow giggled.

"*Jah*, then I'll be the one to blame."

Willow nodded. "Exactly."

Once they had the food in front of them, Lily said, "Now we should say a prayer."

As the girls closed their eyes, they said their silent prayer of thanks for the food. Then they wasted no time eating.

"What's the *boppli* like?" Willow asked.

"Small and cute. When are you going to see her?"

"Whenever Aunt Nancy lets me."

"I'm glad our mothers are getting along better. It's been good having you and Violet here. It would've been very quiet without you now that Daisy's gone."

"Are you missing Daisy?"

"*Nee.*" Lily shook her head, not wanting to admit that she was missing her twin dreadfully. But even if Daisy were there, things wouldn't be the same. They hadn't been the same since Daisy met Bruno. He was now the main person in Daisy's life, so how could things ever be the same?

"Now all your sisters are married," Willow said, chomping on a piece of buttered bread.

"*Denke* for pointing that out."

"I'm just saying that because I think your *mudder* wants you to get married."

"That would be right. She wants to get rid of me out of the *haus*. I've got a job now, so I'm out most of the time. That should keep her happy."

"Why would she want you out of the house all the time?"

"Probably because I annoy her."

"I haven't noticed that you annoy her," Willow said. "This is your home. If anyone's annoying her it might be me and Violet."

"*Nee*, she loves you two." Lily shrugged her shoulders and kept eating. Then she said, "I don't know, she might want to turn the house into a bed and breakfast since it's got seven bedrooms."

Willow giggled. "You're so funny, Lily."

"Well, we do have a lot of bedrooms. When I move out, it's just going to be *Mamm* and *Dat* rattling around in this huge place."

"They might get a smaller one. Or you could marry someone and they could live in your *grossdaddi haus*." Willow giggled again.

"I don't think I'd like that. I think I'd prefer to live with Rose or one of the boys. Anyway, they're hardly old enough for that. Maybe in about thirty years."

"I'm pleased that Tulip is having a *boppli*."

"Me too. I think she was starting to get a little depressed that our brothers and Rose had them and she had none."

"Well, she'll be happy now." Willow ate some more.

"Everyone will be happy except for me."

"And me too," Willow said.

Lily stared at Willow and had to ask, "Why won't you be happy?"

"The same reason as you."

Lily frowned at her younger cousin. "Please explain?"

"You're so pretty and you're worried that you won't find a man who suits you. But you could have any man you want, I'm sure of it. You should see the way all the men look at you, Lily. I know you don't notice, but I have."

Still frowning, Lily asked, "And you have the same problem?"

"I have a problem, but it's not exactly the same. Boys just don't look at me, so I have the opposite problem, but it's still a problem. I'm just too plain and fat."

"You're not plain or fat, Willow. Everyone your age has a little bit of puppy fat and then you lose it when you get a year or two older."

"That's what *Mamm* calls it—puppy fat—but

what if I don't lose it and I'm fat forever? I don't even eat a lot. So I don't know why I'm so fat."

"You're not." She was a little bit chubby and she was short, but Lily was convinced a year or two would fix that problem.

"You're just saying that to be polite. I know that I am, and there's nothing I can do about it."

"You're being far too harsh on yourself."

With her fork, Willow pushed the last morsel of food around on her plate. "I'm being realistic. And that's the best way to be. I don't want to have it in my head that I'm pretty and can get every man like *you* can. But I only need *one* man, I figure."

Lily laughed. "That's what every woman needs—just one man. Just the right one who suits us and doesn't care what we look like."

"Do you honestly think I'll find someone when I get older, Lily?"

"Of course you will, but you don't need to worry about that right now. You've got a long time to go."

"That's all my friends ever talk about—boys."

"You don't need to worry. When the time comes, I'll help you find someone."

"You'd do that for me, Lily?"

"Of course I will. And I'll find you the very best man in the world. *Nee*, wait. I'll have the very best man and I'll find you the second best man in the world. Will that do?"

"*Jah.*" Willow giggled. "*Denke*, Lily."

Lily giggled along with her. "Let's have another helping. There'll still be plenty for them."

"Okay." Willow held out her plate for another serving.

After they ate, the girls washed their dishes and waited in the living room for everyone to come home.

"Now my back is starting to hurt again. I think I need heat on it all the time."

"Do you want a hot water bottle again?"

*"Jah, denke."*

When Lily came back into the living room after making a hot water bottle, she saw Willow yawning. "Do you want to go to bed? You'll be warmer."

*"Jah*, I think I might."

"Do you want a cup of hot tea?"

"You're spoiling me, Lily."

Lily laughed. *"Nee* I'm not. I'm just looking after you and nothing more. That's what *Mamm* told me to do."

"Okay. A hot tea would be lovely. Can you bring it up to my bedroom?"

*"Jah.* You go to bed and I'll bring up the hot tea. I've already got the boiling water."

Willow headed up to bed.

All by herself, Lily headed to the kitchen to make the hot tea. It was odd to have so few people in the house that once had been filled with the talk and laughter of six children. Now that her older siblings had all married, things were so different. If only she could turn back the clock to before Rose married. She and Daisy had so much fun back then. They were always laughing about one thing or another.

## Chapter Ten

Nancy was upset that the girls had squabbled in front of Rose and her newborn baby. It certainly wasn't what Rose needed just after hours of labor. She didn't even know which one was at fault, Tulip or Lily. Lily didn't like to be reminded that Daisy was married and in Ohio, and Tulip just needed some attention.

Understandably, Tulip being the second oldest felt she missed attention when she was growing up. Rose had gotten the attention of the firstborn, and when Tulip was a toddler, the twins arrived. The twins had demanded double the time and attention and it wasn't their fault. Two babies had been so much more work than one. Normally Tulip was mild mannered and calm, but now Nancy could see that she'd have to do something to make Tulip feel special. But how to do that while still giving

Rose and her baby attention and having enough energy left over to look after the cousins while Nerida was still unwell?

Nancy sighed as she sat on the edge of Rose's bed. If only she could split herself into three people.

"What's wrong, *Mamm*?" Rose asked.

Nancy smiled. "Nothing. Everything is right. I'm surrounded by *familye* and I couldn't be happier. You've given me a *wunderbaar grosskin* and soon Tulip is giving me another." Nancy looked at Tulip to see her smile. "Tulip, how pleased was Wilhem when he heard the news?"

"He's the happiest he's ever been. He called all his relatives today as soon as he knew I was planning on telling you all today. Oh, I should've told you when *Dat* was here too, so everyone would hear together. I was just so excited. I've been bursting to tell the news."

"He'll be here soon. You can be the one to tell him," Nancy said.

"I should've waited for one of the family dinners, but I couldn't wait any longer or I'd simply burst."

Everyone laughed.

"We wouldn't want that," Nancy said.

"It'll be the best day of your life. The day your child is born," Rose said.

"*Jah*, I'm so looking forward to it."

"Here's *Onkel* Hezekiah now," Violet said, looking out the window.

"I'll bring him up to the room and you can tell him your news, Tulip."

"And bring Mark as well. He'll be excited that Sarah will have a cousin so close in age," Rose said.

When Rose's husband and Tulip's father were in the room, Tulip repeated her good news.

"That's *wunderbaar*," Hezekiah said.

"I know." Tulip nodded.

"Congratulations, Tulip," Mark said as he looked at Rose. "Did you know?"

"I only just found out."

They stayed talking for a while and then since Hezekiah came in his buggy, Tulip left by herself and Nancy and Violet went home in Hezekiah's buggy.

Just as they were halfway up the driveway to the house, Nancy said, "I'm pleased I've already got the dinner cooked and in the oven. I didn't realize we'd be out this late."

"We'll have to hope that they've left some for us," Violet said.

Nancy laughed. "*Jah*, I hope so. We made enough of it, didn't we?"

"Yeah, I think so."

"It'll be bread and dripping for us if they've eaten it all," Nancy said.

"I'll give that a miss," Hezekiah said, pulling up at the house.

"Do you want me to help you with the horse and buggy, *Onkel* Hezekiah?"

"I'm used to doing it on my own *denke*, Violet."

Violet and Nancy walked into the house, leaving Hezekiah to tend to the horse. Lily was on the couch warming herself by the fire and Willow was nowhere to be seen.

"Where's Willow?" Violet asked.

Lily jumped up and faced them. "She was feeling a bit sore and she's gone to bed early with the hot water bottle. Before that she had a hot bath."

"I thought she would've recovered by now. Did you put some more balm on for her?" Nancy asked Lily.

"I completely forgot about it."

Nancy nodded. "Maybe we should take her to the doctor if she's not any better."

"Okay."

Nancy headed to the kitchen to get the dinner ready and saw that the table was set with three places. She stepped back into the living room. "Did you set the table, Lily?"

"I had to do something while I was waiting for you."

"That's a lovely surprise."

"You didn't eat all the dinner then?" Violet asked.

Lily giggled. "I was thinking of it, but there was too much there." Lily followed her mother into the kitchen while Violet went upstairs to wash up.

"How was Tulip in the end? Was she feeling a bit better by the time you left?"

"I think so. I don't know what got into her tonight. I think she's feeling a bit left out or overlooked."

"She's never felt like that before."

"Perhaps she's feeling a little bit more sensitive now. Pregnancy can do that to a person."

Lily grimaced. "Rose's personality didn't change."

"Everyone is different."

# Chapter Eleven

Nancy walked into Willow's bedroom since she was late coming downstairs for breakfast. She had the covers over her head. Pulling the covers back, Nancy leaned over her. "Are you okay?"

Willow opened her eyes and squinted from the light. "I'm quite sore."

"That's only normal since you had such a hard fall. Do you need help getting dressed?"

"I think I can do it."

"Perhaps we should go to the doctor."

"*Nee*, not the doctor. I'll be fine. As you said, nothing's broken. All the doctor will do is give me a script for painkillers and maybe something to rub into my shoulder."

"I'll mix up another potion. That should help. I'll try something different this time. I'll see you downstairs when you're ready. It'll take me only a few minutes or so to mix up the balm. I used to have it on hand when the boys were young."

"*Denke*, Aunt Nancy."

"I use the one with chamomile and wintergreen oil. The boys always had some kind of injury." Her mind drifted off to days gone by as she remembered how the boys had one injury after another, from falling out of trees to getting fishing hooks stuck through their feet. She looked back at Willow. "Would you like to visit your *Mamm* today?"

Willow shook her head. "She'll find out about my fall and she'll worry."

"Okay. You're probably right. Even if we kept it from her she'd smell the wintergreen and figure out you're sore somewhere."

"She finds out everything."

Nancy gave a little laugh. That's what her daughters always said about her.

"I'll have to visit her soon and tell her about Tulip's exciting news."

"You told her about Rose's *boppli*, *jah*?"

"*Jah*, I called your parents when it was daylight, from Rose's *haus*."

"You could visit her today if you want. Tell her Violet and I are doing plenty of chores to help out. She'll be happy about that."

"You wouldn't mind if I stop by and see her today? I'll only be an hour or so."

"I wouldn't mind. *Mamm* would like it if you went to see her and told her the good news."

"That's a good idea. I'll do that after I cook your breakfast."

"You don't have to cook me breakfast, Aunt Nancy. I can get my own. I'm fine now."

Nancy shook her head. "Your *mudder* wanted you here so I'd look after you and that's what I'll do. I'll cook your breakfast and then I will visit your mother and I'll just have to hope she doesn't get too suspicious and ask why you and Violet aren't with me."

"She'll be so happy about Rose's *boppli* and about Tulip expecting as well."

"I hope so."

"She will be."

"I'll stop by and see if Rose's doing okay before I see Nerida. The midwife's going there today too and she's got Mark, but a girl needs her *mudder* sometimes. That's why I thought you might need yours."

"*Nee*, I'm fine, truly."

Later that day, Nancy left her two nieces at home and traveled to her sister's house. She was weary from having hardly any sleep, but she had things to do and had to keep going. After ten minutes of the horse trotting along the road, her head nodded and she jolted awake. She'd fallen asleep for a few seconds. The only cure she could think of to keep herself awake was to sing a hymn. There was no one around to hear her, so it didn't matter that she couldn't hold a tune and had a terrible voice.

The song did the job of filling her lungs with oxygen and giving her some more energy.

As soon as she stopped the buggy at the house, John came out to see her. "How is she today, John?"

John stroked his long gray beard. "About the same, Nancy. She's feeling sorry for herself and wants to do more than the doctor says she's able."

"Surely she can walk around on crutches or with a walking stick?"

"Maybe soon. Come in and see her."

She walked with John into the house and was surprised to see Nerida propped up by pillows on the couch.

Nerida looked up and saw her. She knew by Nerida's face that she was a welcome sight. "Ah, at last, a visitor."

Nancy laughed. "I would've visited sooner if I knew you wanted to see people so badly."

"Anything to stop the boredom."

She nodded her head toward the couch. "So, this is your new bed?"

"It is now until I can get up the stairs."

"*Jah*, I didn't think about that," Nancy said.

"How are the girls?" Nerida asked.

"The girls are good, really good. I have some news for you, some really good news."

"You've already told us about Rose's *boppli*."

"It's not that. It's Tulip. She's expecting."

Nerida went quiet and put her fingertips to her eyes. "That's such good news. I don't normally cry so easily." She sniffed.

"*Nee*, you don't cry easily. I can't even count on one hand the amount of times I've seen you cry."

"I'm so happy for you and Hezekiah. You've been blessed with so many *grosskinner*."

"I know. It seemed to happen all of a sudden. We had none and then we had one and now we've got quite a few."

"You'll have a lot more too, once Daisy has a couple."

Nancy stared at Nerida and hoped that she wasn't resentful or jealous. "You'll have some too, when your girls get married."

"I know and I'm looking forward to it." Nerida smiled and then she looked over at John, who was standing in the doorway. "Did you hear that, John? You'll soon have another niece or nephew from Wilhem and Tulip."

"*Wunderbaar.* Another blessing *Gott* has bestowed upon you and Hezekiah, Nancy, and us."

Nancy smiled. "We're grateful for every one of them."

"John, can you make Nancy a cup of hot tea?"

"Coming up." He headed to the kitchen.

Nancy bounded to her feet. "I can do it."

"You sit down, Nancy. I've found a few skills I didn't know I had since Nerida has been off her feet."

Nancy sat back down. "Okay." She turned to Nerida. "Do you have any sewing you can do?"

"*Jah*, I've got reading, I've got sewing, I've got my sampler needlework." Nerida sighed. "Things could have been worse."

"I know. I got such a fright to hear you'd fallen off the roof. That is very dangerous."

"*Nee*, I told you, that's something I do all the time. I'd never fallen before."

"You'll never do it again, then, will you?" Nancy stared at Nerida until she shook her head. "Are you certain?"

"I'm certain I won't do it again. I give you my word. I'd like to do something though. Everywhere I look there's something that needs to be cleaned. I'm sitting here looking at the curtains that haven't been washed for two months. I just want to get up and wash them." Her gaze lowered. "And look at this floor."

"It looks fine to me," Nancy said.

"I can see dust everywhere."

"Well, stop looking for it. When things calm down a bit at home, I'll come and clean for you."

"What's going on at home?"

Nancy had to think fast. The last thing she needed was for Nerida to worry about Willow. "It's just that Lily has started work at the flower stall where Rose used to work, and Rose has just had the baby, so I'll have to be over there lending her a hand every day. Then there are just lots of little things that keep cropping up."

"If my girls are too much trouble, just send them back."

John came out from the kitchen with the tea. "You should have complete rest, Nerida. Nancy told you she doesn't mind having the girls."

"That's all I've been doing. Resting, resting, resting."

"The girls are no trouble. I love having them there, and they've been such great company for Lily. She misses Daisy. I know she loves having them there too. And the girls all get along so well."

"Are you sure?" Nerida asked.

"I'm quite sure," Nancy said as John handed her a cup of tea. "*Denke*, John. Are either of you having tea?"

"We've only just had one," John said.

"I wouldn't have had one if I knew that neither of you were having one."

"That's okay, John doesn't mind. Now what else has been going on in the community? Rose's baby has just been born, and Tulip's expecting, so is there anything else you haven't told me about?"

"I can't think of anything."

"Has Lily got a boyfriend yet?"

"*Nee*, and she's my next project. I'm monitoring the situation closely."

Nerida looked over at her husband who had just walked into the kitchen. She whispered to Nancy, "Who do you think is a good match for Lily?"

"I have my eyes on two men. Matthew, Mark's brother, and Elijah Bontrager."

Nerida slowly nodded.

"Which one do you prefer?" Nancy asked.

"I don't know them well enough. The Bontragers keep to themselves really, and Matthew seems a little young. I can see Lily with an older man. Maybe Elijah would be good."

"I'd be happy if she married either one of them."

"What does she think about them?" Nerida leaned forward.

"That's the problem, Nerida. Lily doesn't think."

Nerida covered her mouth with her hand and giggled. "Oh, Nancy, you're dreadful."

Nancy laughed along with her. Being with her sister was just like old times in their pre-rift days. They were getting along as though nothing had ever happened.

* * *

Lily figured the proper thing to do was to make amends with Tulip. She wanted her to know that she was genuinely happy for her and that's why she made up her mind to visit Tulip after she briefly stopped by Mark and Rose's to take them the bread and potatoes they needed. While she was there, she had a quick hold of baby Sarah. Then her two older brothers arrived with their wives, giving Lily the perfect excuse to leave and see Tulip.

As she stepped down from the buggy outside Tulip's house, she saw Tulip opening the front door. "Hello." Lily waved as she looped the reins over the fence.

"Hi," Tulip called back. "Is everything okay?"

"*Jah*, I just thought I'd stop by." When she got closer, she said, "I just wanted to say I'm sorry for the argument we had."

"That's okay. Come inside. Do you want something to eat or maybe some coffee?"

"*Nee denke*. I'm just on my way home from work."

She knew from the look on Tulip's face that she was pleased. She continued, "*Mamm's* got such a lot on with Willow hurting her shoulder, Aunt Nerida sick and now Rose's *boppli*."

"*Jah*, I know, but I feel it's always the same. I'm always missing out. If all that hadn't happened,

*Mamm* would've been over here fussing over me and making sure I have everything I need."

"What do you need? I can get you anything you need."

They both sat on the couch as Tulip giggled. "I don't mean it like that. I just mean that, oh, it's hard to explain. Anyway, I don't need anyone to make a fuss, but it is my first *boppli*, so it's kind of a special time for me and I just would've liked everybody to be happy for me."

"Everyone is happy for you."

"I guess."

"Anyway, you have a husband to fuss over you now."

"I know and he's been really good."

"Have you had morning sickness?" Lily asked.

"*Nee*, and I'm pleased about that."

"Show me how fat you are." Lily leaned forward and pressed Tulip on her stomach.

"Stop it!" Tulip smacked her hand away.

"I was only checking."

"I'm hardly fat at all. It's too early to tell."

"Rose was fat when she was four months."

Tulip giggled again. "That's only because she's so skinny normally."

"True." Lily was hoping she was cheering Tulip up.

"Have you heard from Daisy?"

"*Nee. Mamm* told me that Daisy told her she

was going to write and she hasn't. She's having too much fun with Bruno, I suppose."

"*Jah*, I guess. It's hard. I mean, don't be too upset with her. She's a newlywed and they naturally want to spend time with each other."

"I noticed. She's got no time for me at all."

"That'll change and you'll be her closest friend again. She'll need you more than ever soon. Just wait until she gets back and gets settled into a daily routine."

Lily nodded and hoped Tulip was right, but she'd come to make Tulip feel better. "I want to sew your *boppli* some clothes, or even knit something."

"You don't have to do that. I know you don't like sewing or knitting."

"I do. It'll be fun. And making small clothes, they'd be done in no time."

"Okay, if you want to."

"I do. Do you think you'll have a boy or a girl?"

"A girl, I think. I had a dream about a girl."

"Just one? Not twins?"

Tulip covered her mouth and giggled. "Just one. I don't think I'd be able to handle the double trouble of twins."

"It wouldn't be so bad. I'd like it."

"Perhaps *Gott* will bless you or Daisy with twins."

"*Jah*, I think so. What time does Wilhem get home?"

"In another hour."

Lily nodded, wondering what else to say. It was hard without Daisy. Their conversation had always been bounced off the other's. "I'm so happy about your *boppli*, Tulip."

"Me too. I thought I was never going to get pregnant and I'd almost given up hope. My miracle came when I wasn't expecting it."

"I should get home. I've had a long day." Lily stretched her arms over her head and yawned. It was hard being on her feet most of the day.

"*Denke* for stopping by, Lily." Tulip reached over and gave Lily a hug.

Lily felt good about visiting Tulip. She'd been so close to Daisy that she sometimes hadn't appreciated her other two sisters. With Daisy gone, she was able to see that.

## Chapter Twelve

Lily walked in the door, glad to be home. Lately, it had been one tiring day after another. When she noticed a letter waiting for her on the table just inside the front door, her mood altered dramatically. Her mother and father received letters all the time, but no one ever wrote to her directly. The letter had to be from Daisy.

After she'd grabbed the letter, she stared at the carefully executed L of her first name. A wide scroll at the top of the L was extenuated by an equal sized loop in the corner of the L. The Y of Yoder was just as scrolled and wonderful. Lily giggled out loud when she pictured the concentration on her twin sister's face as she, with head bent over inches from the envelope, labored over producing the wonderfully crafted letters which would've had to have been just so. Daisy was fairly haphazard about most things, but writing was something that she was careful about.

Lily plummeted from elation to devastation in seconds when she realized that the letter might not hold good news. If Daisy was coming home as soon as she'd said, then why was she writing at all? Did the letter hold news that Daisy and Bruno had decided to stay in Ohio?

While the letter was still clutched in her hand, her mother walked out of the kitchen and looked her up and down. Her mother's smile turned into a frown as she looked at Lily standing with the letter clutched to herself.

"Oh, you found that letter? It came today."

"Is this going to be bad news, *Mamm*? Did she send a letter to you as well?"

"*Nee*, she didn't."

She held the letter up to the light. "I hope this doesn't mean she's going to stay there longer."

"How long are you going to wait to see what it says? Open it up."

"I'm terrified of what information the letter holds."

"Oh, Lily, why do you always think everything is going to be bad?" Her mother's green eyes fixed onto her, making Lily feel foolish.

"Lately, everything is, that's why. I never used to have to think like that. Now it just saves more disappointment if I expect the worst."

"You're being silly. Go on. Open it!"

Lily took off her black shawl and hung it on the peg by the door. Then, with shoulders drooped, she headed to the couch and flopped down onto it. She didn't know what she would do if her twin had written to tell her she wasn't coming home. There was a strong possibility that Daisy might be staying in Ohio with the rest of Bruno's family. It seemed that Bruno's only family member who did not live in Ohio was Valerie. Valerie had resisted all attempts by Bruno to make her go back there with him, but what if all his talk had worked on Daisy?

She stared at the letter. When she finally ripped it open, she was further upset to see that the letter was only one page, and not only that, Daisy had only written on half of that one page.

She ran her eyes along every carefully written line. Daisy explained that she was staying on a little longer with Bruno while he sorted out things in regard to his horse business. Daisy had suggested that Lily come there to visit. There wasn't much else in Daisy's letter—nothing to allay Lily's fears about losing Daisy to Ohio forever. Now, she was surer than ever that Bruno was deliberately delaying her coming back to Lancaster County. Why would Daisy suggest she visit unless she was going to be there for a long time? Maybe she'd never see Daisy again.

Her patient mother finally leaned forward. "Well, what did she say?"

Lily passed the letter over. "There's not much to it."

Her mother read the letter and then handed it back. "She said she's coming home as soon as Bruno tends to a few things. That was good of her to let us know."

"Can we trust him, though, *Mamm*?"

Her mother laughed, but it wasn't a real laugh. It was more of a nervous cackle. "Do you think Bruno has some devious plan to steal Daisy away from us?"

"It happens. Anyway, she might think she doesn't need us now that she's got Bruno. She certainly stopped talking to me as much when Bruno came along. We were so close and then she dumped me for a man. I would've never done that to her. Things will never be the same. She's got Bruno, but I've got no one now."

"You've still got Daisy. You'll always have her."

Lily pushed out her bottom lip.

"You've got your *vadder* and me."

Staring at her mother, Lily wondered what to say to that. It wasn't the same. She couldn't talk to them as she'd talked to Daisy. It wasn't so much the talking; it was the laughing and the fun they'd had together and the pranks they'd played. *"Denke, Mamm."*

"Cheer up."

Lily nodded, wondering if Daisy missed her at all.

"What you need is to get married. When you find your own husband, you won't miss Daisy so much."

Her mother thought everyone needed to get married and the sooner, the better. She didn't understand her at all. Losing Daisy was traumatic and only someone who was a twin could understand. There was no fix for what she felt, no Band-Aid that could be placed across her emptiness. Only having Daisy back would fix things, but that was never going to happen. "I'd rather have Daisy back. The old Daisy, not the person she turned into when she met Bruno." She shook her head in disgust. "He's got a lot to answer for."

"Bruno is a lovely man and he's done nothing wrong."

Lily nodded again. The best way to keep her mother quiet was to pretend that she agreed with her. "You're right, *Mamm*. I'm sorry."

"Now go and wash up and then you can help me with dinner."

When her mother hurried back to the kitchen, Lily trudged up the stairs with Daisy's letter in her hand. She closed her bedroom door, and then slumped down on her bed to read the letter over again, more carefully this time. After reading it the second time, she felt no better. She bounded to her feet and ripped the letter into small pieces. So her mother wouldn't know what she'd done, she shoved the pieces into the top drawer of her chest of drawers. Sometimes her mother came into her room with clean folded clothes, but she'd always place them on top of her bed. She'd never have reason to look in her drawers.

Once she'd closed the drawer with force, she muttered, "That's what I think of you, Daisy Yoder." She headed back downstairs to wash up while she told herself she'd never change when she fell in love—and if she did, it would be a change for the better.

Stepping into the kitchen, she saw Willow and Violet helping her mother scrape the peelings from the vegetables. It was as though her cousins had replaced herself and Daisy. At least they were doing some of the chores that she might have had to do.

After she'd slumped into a chair at the kitchen table, her mother stared at her. "Have you washed your hands?"

"Not yet."

"Well, go on."

"I just got home. Can I have a minute to rest?"

Willow and Violet giggled at Lily while she stared at the flowers from Elijah. The flowers had opened further and were more beautiful than when she'd brought them home. She leaned over and

*Amish Lily*

breathed in their sweet, fresh perfume. Elijah had been about to ask her something at the ice-skating right before Willow had the accident. Would she ever find out what it was? Or had the moment passed forever? She sat back heavily in the chair, trying her hardest not to be mad at Willow.

"How are you feeling, Willow?" Lily asked.

"I'm better now, *denke*."

"That's good." Lily looked up at her mother, who was glaring at her. "Okay, I'm going. I thought you would've given me a free pass from chores tonight."

"I never get a pass. Everyone has to eat. You'll find that out when you become a *mudder* yourself. Then you'll know how hard it is to run a household. Not that I'm complaining. It's just that you just don't know how much it takes."

As Lily walked out of the room to wash her hands, her mother called after her, "We need your help. The sooner we get the dinner cooked, the sooner we can all eat."

"And the sooner I can go to bed and get some peace," Lily called back, risking her mother's temper.

The cousins giggled at her again.

## Chapter Thirteen

The next day, Lily was engrossed in a conversation with Matthew about his new venture when she looked over her shoulder and saw Elijah heading toward them.

Matthew turned around when he saw Lily looking at something. "Here's Elijah again. He hasn't come here to see me." Matthew backed away and headed back to his stall.

"Hello, Elijah."

"I'm between jobs at the moment. I've had one across town and I've got one close by and I'm due to be there in fifteen minutes—I have to be quick. I just came to ask you if you'd have dinner with me tonight?"

Out of the corner of her eye, Lily saw that Matthew was far enough away that he wouldn't be able to hear what was being said. "*Jah*, I'd like that."

His eyes glistened. "Shall I come by your house at six thirty?"

"That sounds good."

"See you then." After he flashed her a smile, he hurried away.

"Again, he ignored me," Matthew called out to Lily when Elijah had gone.

Lily looked over at Matthew and laughed. Her whole world lit up when Elijah was around. She kept to herself what Elijah had asked her. It was no one's business but their own.


When Lily got home, her mother and the cousins were sitting at the kitchen table peeling the vegetables for the evening meal.

"I won't be having dinner here tonight, *Mamm*."

"Oh? Where will you be having it?"

"I'm going out with Elijah tonight."

The cousins just looked at each other as though it was news to them that she liked Elijah.

"How is your shoulder today, Willow, still good?"

"It's much better. Your mother has been putting her special balm on it and it's helped a lot."

"That's good. I'm glad to hear that stuff actually works. If it had been me, I would've gotten something from the pharmacy."

Lily's mother picked up a peeling knife and shook it at Lily. "It does the same thing, Lily. You'll be paying a lot of money at the pharmacy for something, and what's the point in that?"

Violet added, "*Jah*, and why pay money for something we can make at home?"

"You'll make someone a *gut fraa* someday, Violet."

Violet smiled at Nancy's words.

"Violet already has more sense than you, Lily," her mother said.

Lily's jaw dropped open. "I was just making a comment. I didn't wanna have an argument about it." Lily turned on her heel and walked out of the room.

She had no time to be upset over her mother's words. She had to get ready for tonight. Besides, she doubted her mother meant what she said. She was most likely trying to make Violet feel good about herself.

Wondering what to wear for her date, Lily felt her heart pound against her chest. She had to look her best. Would he propose? Was it too early for that? *It would be nice to be married close in time to Daisy and then our kinner might be the same age.* To Lily, that slightly made up for the fact that they hadn't married brothers as they'd planned.

Lily made sure she was ready and waiting when Elijah arrived on the dot of six thirty. She hurried out to meet him, not wanting the awkwardness and embarrassment of him coming into the house and saying hello to everybody. The cousins would most likely gawk at him or giggle.

"Hello, Lily. Are you ready to go?"

"I am." She climbed into the buggy and sat beside him. They set off. Giving him a sideways glance, she noticed that he'd also taken some care to dress well and with the faintest aroma of lavender in the air, she knew he'd freshly showered using lavender soap.

Elijah was the first to speak when they left the long driveway and turned onto the road. "I've been meaning to talk with you for some time, but it's hard with so many people constantly around you. Even at the market you've got people coming and going, and also Matthew at the next stall who can probably hear everything we say."

"I know it's hard to talk privately. I never get a moment to myself at home either now with the cousins there."

Elijah continued, "I figured the only way we could have a real talk is if I took you for dinner somewhere."

"I'm always ready to eat." Lily gave a little giggle and wondered if she should've said something about the company rather than eating.

"I'm taking you to an old Amish farmhouse that's been converted into a restaurant. I've heard good things, but I've never been there before."

"Does it have Amish food?"

"*Jah*, supposedly traditional Amish food."

"I'll have to see if it's as nice as *Mamm's* cooking."

When they walked into the restaurant, the first thing Lily noticed was the color of the walls. She'd never seen red walls, but they worked so well with the rustic light-colored wooden floors and the Amish farmyard murals. To one side of the room were three long counters where people were helping themselves to the smorgasbord. Three rows of pendant lights hung above the food counters while the lighting in the rest of the room was more subdued. A waiter showed them to their seats at one of the three rows of rustic wooden tables.

Lily had thought Elijah would take her somewhere a little more intimate since he'd made that speech about wanting to speak with her in private.

Once they sat, they looked at each other.

"Well, we best go and get some food," he said.

She agreed, and then they took a dinner plate each and walked down each counter, every now and then taking whatever took their fancy. There were red beets, chicken, ham loaf, chow chow, whipped potatoes, and several different kinds of roast vegetables, as well as plenty of fresh bread, whipped butter, and gravy.

Before Lily sat down again, she cast her eyes over the desserts and hoped she'd still have room.

There were pies of all kinds, shoo fly pies, and ice-cream and cream.

"A lot of this is traditional food I haven't seen for some time."

"Me too," he said as they sat down.

After they'd eaten a few mouthfuls, Elijah said, "I suppose I should get right down to the point of why I asked you here." He put his knife and fork down and placed his elbows on the table. "It's a hard thing to say."

"The best way to do it is to say it quickly."

"That's one of the things I like about you, Lily. You're so forthright."

"Isn't it the best way to be?"

"It is. I want to be straightforward with you because you've always been that way with me. With you, it's what you see is what you get. There's nothing hidden."

She was pleased he liked the way that she was because many people didn't; she was certain of that. Noticing he wasn't smiling, she no longer thought he'd brought her there to propose. Or was he simply working up the nerve to ask if they could be boyfriend and girlfriend? Surely he knew she'd be happy about that. Why was he looking so sad?

Finally, she said, "You don't have to tell me right away. I can wait. We haven't even finished dinner yet."

"It's something…it's hard for me to say."

"Just say it."

He nodded and then looked into her eyes. "The thing, Lily…" He stopped, and then started again. "You see, the thing is that we've been kind of growing closer over the past few months and you've become very important to me. You're someone I like to be around very much. And I've come to think that you feel the same way about me."

She nodded. "I do. I feel that way too."

"There's something you don't know about me."

A knot formed in Lily's stomach. What could it possibly be?

# Chapter Fourteen

Lily swallowed hard. Hearing Elijah tell her from his own lips that there was something she didn't know about him filled her with fear. She placed her knife and fork down because she could feel her hands trembling. "What don't I know?" Her heart pumped hard and she could feel the vibration of her heart thumping in her head.

"Many years ago, I pledged my word that I would marry a girl from a community in Lowville. My parents knew her family very well, and that's where we lived before we came here after my mother died."

Lily sat frozen to her chair, wondering if she was having a bad dream. Now his hesitance in getting to know her better made sense. It had annoyed her, at the beginning of getting to know him, that he didn't pay her as much attention as the other young men did. "Are you joking?"

"I'm serious. I planned to move there within a year."

"What, to marry this girl simply because her parents once knew your parents or something?"

"It's not the way you said." He shook his head. "I didn't explain it well."

Lily breathed out heavily and folded her arms tightly against her chest.

When he looked up at her, he continued, "The thing is, how it all came about doesn't matter so much. I've given my word that I'll marry her. She knows it, and her whole family knows it and so does mine."

"How long ago did you give your word?"

"Quite a while ago."

Lily shook her head, barely able to take it all in. "Do you want to marry her?"

"I don't. Not now I don't. Not now that I've met you."

"They can't make you do it."

"No one is making me. I can't go back on my word. I didn't know that you'd come along. Patricia and I have kept in touch and she wants this to go ahead."

"And you haven't met with her recently?"

He shook his head. "I just wanted to tell you how things were before things get too difficult.

After I met you, I regretted my decision, but as a man of *Gott*, I can't go back on my word. That would be lying and letting people down."

Now Lily was the one staring down at the table. What about letting her down? "Why did you buy me the flowers and say all those things to me?"

"I shouldn't have let my feelings carry me away. It was wrong of me to carry on our friendship."

Elijah was the only man she could see herself married to and now he'd swiftly pulled the rug out from underneath her. She studied his face and saw how troubled he was. She respected that he couldn't go back on his word and he wouldn't be Elijah if he didn't do what he believed to be right. One of the things she liked about him was his goodness. "When do you leave for Lowville?"

"There's no exact timeframe for me to go. I figured on helping my *vadder* in his business for another few months before I head off."

Lily heaved out a sigh. Things had never worked out for her and now she knew she wasn't going to find the right man and have a happy marriage just as her sisters had.

Shaking her head, she said quietly, "I can't believe they would hold you to such a thing."

"I gave my word, Lily. If I had known I was going to meet you, I wouldn't have made that commitment. The decision's been made. As I said, I never expected to feel about someone the way I feel

about you. Everything about you is delightful—
your humor, your energy and your zest for life…"
His voice trailed off.

She looked across at him. "But all that isn't
enough?"

"I'm explaining things to you the best that I
can."

She lowered her head again. Tears escaped
from her eyes and she couldn't stop them. Soon
her cheeks were wet with tears. Wiping the mois-
ture from her face with the back of her hand, she
stood. "I have to go."

"We'll go." He leaped to his feet and took hold
of her arm, and together they walked out the restaurant door and hurried back to his buggy.

Once he got into the driver's seat beside her, he
said, "I never meant it to happen this way. It was a
mistake to take you to a restaurant. I don't know
what I was thinking."

She shook her head. "You weren't to know I'd
cry like a fool."

"You're not a fool, Lily. You're a wonderful
and amazing woman. I'm the fool for making a
commitment before I was mature enough to know
what an impact that could have. I didn't know what
love… I can't say more out of respect for my future wife."

Hearing him say the words 'future wife' upset
her even more. She steeled her heart and sniffed

back her tears, telling herself she could cry all she liked once she got back home and was safely in her bedroom.

"I'll take you home, but shall we at least get some take-out? I don't want you going hungry."

"Okay." Lily agreed because she didn't want him to know how devastated she was by the news. It had been the last thing she'd expected him to say. If only she hadn't expected him to propose.

They went through the drive-through of the local burger restaurant and ordered fries and burgers.

"I'll eat mine at home," Lily said when he passed her the food.

"Okay. I'll wait before I eat mine too."

They journeyed to Lily's house in silence while Lily did her best not to think about anything to prevent further tears. Part of her was angry with Elijah for being so silly. She'd always thought he was sensible, but promising himself in marriage with someone he didn't love was foolhardy. The other part of her was angry with herself for falling in love with him.

By the time they got to her house, Lily was so upset she thought she'd be sick. With the food on her lap, she sat fiddling nervously with her prayer *kapp* until Elijah took her hand into his own and gave it a reassuring squeeze.

"Everything will turn out well for you, Lily."

"How can you know that?"

"You're wonderful. How could it not?"

Lily nodded and forced herself to smile while her insides tumbled.

Nothing made sense. Why did God let this man into her life only to take him away? It was cruel to offer someone something and then snatch it away. It was like showing a hungry person a bowl of food only to tip it out at their feet.

"I'm glad you told me this now, Elijah."

"I didn't know when the right time would be. It would've been weird to tell you sooner because I wasn't certain how you felt about me, but as we got closer..."

"There's no need to explain." She pulled her hand back, and then stepped down from the buggy with the take-out bag tucked under her arm. "I guess I'll see you 'round, Elijah." It was her fault for pursuing him so relentlessly. She knew that now.

He nodded and, with longing in his eyes, said, "Goodbye, Lily."

She gave a little nod as she couldn't say more, and then she turned and made her way to the house. The clip-clop of the buggy horse rang out behind her as she opened the front door. After she took off her shawl and hung it on the peg, she stepped further inside to see four pairs of eyes staring at her in silence. Her parents and her cousins were sitting in the living room.

"You're early, Lily. We didn't expect you…" Then her mother saw her face.

Lily knew she looked a dreadful mess, no doubt with swollen red eyes and a ruddy face. "Who wants this?" She stretched out the paper bag toward the cousins. "It's burgers and fries."

"Who's it for?" Violet asked.

"It was supposed to be mine, but I can't eat." Since neither of the cousins said anything, Lily said, "I'll leave it in the kitchen and whoever wants it can have it."

Her mother jumped up and raced after her, grabbing her by the arm when she'd caught up with her. "Lily, what's wrong?"

Lily pulled her arm back. "It's too hard to explain."

"I know something's wrong. You went out to dinner with Elijah, and went off happily. Now you return early with take-out. What happened, Lily?"

"Everything went wrong. We didn't get along at all, we had a difference of opinion, and he politely got me take-out and drove me home. I'm finished with Elijah Bontrager. We're through!"

Her mother raised a quizzical eyebrow. "But you always got on with him so well."

"Not anymore."

"Did you have an argument? Sometimes having an argument is a healthy thing to do. It sorts out your differences and then you can put them behind you or find a common ground."

Lily shook her head and tossed the take-out bag on the long wooden table. "Don't look for anything to make sense, *Mamm*, nothing does. We get along fine, but our relationship will never go anywhere and he told me that tonight. I'm just a friend to him."

Her mother's face soured. "I suppose that's best for you to find out now before you developed any real feelings for him."

Lily knew her mother had no idea how she felt or that she'd already fallen in love with Elijah while trying to tell herself she didn't want marriage. Deep in her heart, she wanted to get married, to have her own home and babies, but only with Elijah.

Rubbing her sore eyes, Lily sighed. "I suppose I should get an early night."

"Don't you want to stay up? Your *vadder* was telling the girls stories about when he was young."

Lily untied the strings of her prayer *kapp*. "I've heard them all before."

"So have I, but he tells them so well. I like to listen."

"You listen, then. I'm going up to my room." Lily had only taken two steps away from her mother when her mother spoke.

"How about I bring you up a nice cup of hot tea?"

Lily turned around and gave her mother a tiny smile. "*Denke*, *Mamm*, that'd be *gut*." Her mother always thought that either hot tea or food would solve all life's problems. It was then that Lily spied the roses Elijah had given her. She hurried toward them and picked them out of the vase. With the water dripping from the stems, she marched outside and threw them in the garden.

Walking back inside, she saw her mother staring at her with an open mouth. She grabbed the mop from behind the door and mopped the water droplets from the floor. "I'll rinse the vase tomorrow morning, *Mamm*, and then I'll put it away."

"I'll do that for you, Lily."

*"Denke, Mamm,"* Lily said, hurrying past her mother.

## Chapter Fifteen

Nancy poured the hot tea into the teacup and put a couple of cookies on a plate for Lily. When she was at the bottom of the stairs, Violet came alongside her.

"Would you like me to take that up to Lily, Aunt Nancy?"

"*Nee*, I should do it. I need to have a little chat with her. It's nothing to worry about. She's just a little upset."

"Okay."

Nancy's nieces were quiet, reserved and very polite; nothing like Lily or Daisy. If only Lily had been more like her cousins then things might have gone easier for her. Nancy feared that the path of love would never run easily for her remaining unmarried daughter. And now with her sadness over

Daisy going, things would be harder for Lily all round.

The door of Lily's bedroom was slightly ajar. Nancy leaned her body against it and entered the room to see Lily already in her nightgown, running a brush through her hair as though nothing was wrong. Nancy spotted an uncluttered area on the nightstand and placed the tray down.

"How are you feeling now? A little better?"

"Fine. I'm fine, *Mamm*. I don't know what got into me. I don't know why I was crying. If he's not the right man for me, it has to be someone else."

Nancy sat down on the bed. Her first thought was that Lily was only telling her what she wanted to hear, but giving her the benefit of the doubt, she felt a glimmer of hope that at last Lily was being sensible. "That's right. You'll meet someone else. Elijah just wasn't the right one for you. But I see the way Matthew looks at you and I know he just adores you."

"Which Matthew? I know a few." She knew her mother was referring to Matthew Schumacher, her close friend from the markets who also happened to be her brother-in-law since his older brother was married to her older sister.

"Matthew Schumacher."

"He'll be a good husband for somebody. He's got a lot of good business ideas and he's acting on them, not just talking about them."

"You see? Maybe Matthew's the man for you."

"Maybe."

"Well if you need to talk, I'm always here." Nancy knew it would be hard for Lily to confide in anybody but her twin. Daisy and she had always been close-knit and that was why she'd never had the same bond with the twins as she'd had with her two older daughters. The twins had only ever needed each other.

Nancy stood up, leaned over and kissed Lily on the forehead. "You know, if we can cast all our cares on Him—"

"*Jah*, I know the rest. *Denke*, *Mamm*. I'll pray and everything will be okay."

Her words were glib, but when she glanced at her daughter's face once more, she felt a glimmer of hope that she might have been sincere. "That's the best we can do."

"You've been a *gut mudder* to me."

A surprised giggle escaped Nancy's lips. It was nice to hear.

When her mother left the room, Lily reached over and took the teacup on the nightstand in both hands. The cup was shaking in her trembling hands and she couldn't steady it. It was no use trying to drink it—she was too upset, and what's more, her stomach churned. The cup landed with a clink back on the saucer.

She'd seen a glimpse of true love before it had been snatched away. There were no words to describe how she felt when she was around Elijah. It was as though she wasn't living when he wasn't around. No one else had made her feel like a lantern had been lit inside her.

One by one, she thought about all the men she'd ever liked. Nathanial made her laugh and he was exciting to be around, but could she trust him? Although he was handsome, with rich brown hair and vivid blue-green eyes that stood out against his tanned olive skin, one of the most important things for Lily was to have a man she could trust. Then there was Matthew who was nice as well as trustworthy. He'd be a good provider and he'd be a good father. Out of the various other men she could think of, Matthew stood out in front of them all.

If only Elijah would back out of the arrangement. It was no use; she knew that Elijah was not going to go back on his word. God had to have other plans for her, which meant she would have to forget all about Elijah Bontrager. Why had he bought her those flowers and been so nice to her? It had felt good to throw the flowers away. If Elijah was thinking about marrying someone else, then so should she.

The next day, Lily went to work as though nothing had happened. It was hard to do, but she put on a brave face and did the best she could to forget about Elijah. In between customers, she talked with Matthew and found out more about his business plans. It still seemed unlikely that someone as young as Matthew could have such grand plans. Lily had thought at one time that Tulip and Matthew might become a pair, but it clearly was never to be when Wilhem came on the scene.

Still unable to shake the notion of Elijah married to someone else, on her way home, she stopped at Valerie's house. She had to unload her heavy heart onto someone. Valerie and she had become close in the past months, even though Valerie was closer to her mother in age.

Valerie was also a good friend to Ed Bontrager, Elijah's father. Ed and Valerie had both lost their spouses and appeared to be fond of one another. Lily's mother often had Valerie and Ed and his sons over for dinner. It would be convenient if Ed had mentioned something to Valerie of Elijah's plans and if so, Valerie might be able to tell her more about the situation that Elijah had gotten himself into.

A short time later, Lily sat opposite Valerie, drinking tea.

"Are you sure that's what he said? He's marrying some woman he hardly knows from Lowville?" Valerie asked upon hearing the whole story.

"I wouldn't make a mistake about a thing like that."

"No one has mentioned anything to me, but I never asked. I knew they had some kind of relative or friend who was starting a community up that way somewhere and I heard someone was going to marry someone, but this is the first I've heard that Elijah was going away to marry someone. I always thought you and he—"

Lily cut across her, saying, "I was starting to think that way too. That's why I was so surprised and upset when he told me. He said he was going in less than a year. That means I have to see him for a long time, knowing that he's just going to go off and marry someone else."

"Don't upset yourself. I'm seeing Ed tomorrow. I've offered to make some curtains for his *haus* and I'm meeting him at his home to take some window measurements. I'll ask him about Elijah's plans while I'm there."

"That would be *wunderbaar*, but please don't say that I said anything."

"*Nee*, I won't. I'll work it into the conversation somehow. I'll just say that I've heard talk. I won't tell him more and he might not even ask me."

"*Denke* for doing this for me, Valerie. I don't talk to many people about my secrets now that Daisy has gone."

"You're speaking about her like she's dead.

She'll come back, and when she does, you two will be closer than ever. Don't you worry about a thing."

Lily shook her head. "I don't think we'll ever be close like we once were. I don't think she really cares about me anymore. She doesn't need me because she's got Bruno."

"We all need our sisters, and twins are even more special."

"I have to wait and see, I guess. She seems to have been gone for so long."

"Tomorrow, after I've finished up with Ed, I'll come to the markets and tell you what I've learned."

"That would be *gut*, *denke*. And, that way, we can keep it just between us."

"Exactly."

# Chapter Sixteen

*"Mamm!"* Lily raced into the house and closed the door behind her.

Her mother raced out from the kitchen, wiping her hands on a dishtowel. "What's wrong?"

"Nothing."

"Why are you yelling?" Her mother's hand flew to her heart. "You gave me a dreadful fright."

"Sorry, I just wanted to ask you about something."

"What is it?"

Lily giggled at her mother's face. "Not like this. We have to sit down and have a mother-daughter talk."

"Okay. We haven't done that in a while."

"I'll make us a cup of tea."

While they waited for the pot to boil, they both sat down at the kitchen table.

"I've just been to visit Valerie."

"Did you tell her about what happened between you and Elijah?"

"*Jah*, I did. She won't repeat it. She's become a friend."

Her mother nodded. "I'm glad you find you can talk to her. She's sensible."

"She gave me some good advice."

After Lily got up to make the tea, she pushed a cup toward her mother and sat down with one in front of herself.

"I was wondering if there was ever anything between her and Ed years ago, when they were single."

Her mother frowned. "In what way?"

"Daisy and I often talked about it. We noticed the first time they had dinner here. We sensed something between them."

With a slight raise of her eyebrows, her mother took a polite sip of tea. When she placed the cup back in the saucer she looked across at Lily. "Long ago...and this is only for your ears."

"Of course, I'll never repeat it."

"Long ago, before either of them married, they were friendly."

Lily pulled a face. "What does that mean? They were just friends or something more?"

"It's so long ago that it's hard to remember exactly. I recall thinking at the time that they'd most likely marry, but they didn't. I was a newlywed at the time so I was occupied with other things. Ed was gone for some time and came back with a wife from Lowville."

Lily gasped. "That's where Elijah has to go to get married. That makes sense. He said his mother and father were living in Lowville for some time before they moved here." Lily nodded, trying to fit the pieces together. "How does everything fit in? Didn't Valerie come from Ohio when she married Dirk? Was she ever here before that?"

"Valerie had a friend here that she'd visit once a year."

"Ah. And she would've met Dirk and Ed on her visits."

Her mother nodded and took a sip of tea.

"And how long after Ed got married did Valerie marry Dirk?"

"About a year."

"I wonder if Ed broke her heart."

Her mother leaned toward her. "Did she say anything?"

"*Nee.* I never asked. I would feel awkward asking her anything about Ed. I know they're very friendly." Lily wouldn't tell her mother that Valerie was finding out information about Elijah from Ed, who was Elijah's father. She was sure her mother

might be a little shocked that Valerie was playing along with what she would call one of Lily's
schemes.

Pacing up and down along the front of her
flower stall, Lily wished she had asked Valerie
approximately what time she would be coming. It
was now two in the afternoon. *Perhaps she's forgotten all about it*, Lily thought.

She was immediately relieved when she saw
Valerie hurrying toward her. She glanced over at
Matthew to see that he was busy serving customers and would not hear what was being said. Just
in case, she walked to the farthest edge of the stall
away from Matthew and waited for Valerie.

"What did you find out?" Lily asked when Valerie finally reached her. From the look on Valerie's
face, she knew the news wasn't going to be good.

"It's exactly what you told me. It was an arrangement made some time ago."

The air temporarily left Lily's lungs. "But
surely no one could make him do that—marry
that woman he hardly knows. He told me himself
he's not in love with her. And he told me he regrets
agreeing to the whole thing."

Valerie reached out and placed a comforting
hand on Lily's arm. "No one is aware that he wants
to get out of it."

"He did say it wouldn't be right to go back on his word." Lily bit her lip.

"You have to forget about him, Lily, or you'll drive yourself crazy. You already look a mess."

"There are some who say I'm already crazy, so it doesn't matter much." Lily looked down at her crumpled dress. It was the same dress she'd been wearing the day before. She hadn't even hung it up. It had been in a bundle on the floor all night. Not caring about how she looked, she'd just pulled it on that morning.

"Why don't you come to my place for dinner tonight?"

Lily was relieved at the thought. "That would be good. I don't really want to go home and face everyone. My cousins will ask me so many questions. I just know they will. I've been avoiding them ever since I came home early from my dinner with Elijah."

"I'll have dinner ready and then we can relax and talk."

"You're a good friend, Valerie."

Valerie put her hand to her mouth and gave a little giggle, just as her mother had given a giggle when she'd told her she'd been a good mother.

There had to be some kind of a reason that this was all happening to her. And she was going to start being a better person right now. "What can

I bring for dinner? Would you like me to bring a cake for dessert?"

"I have so much food at home. Just bring yourself."

As soon as Valerie left, Matthew walked over to her. "You two seemed to be having an in-depth conversation."

"She invited me to dinner tonight."

Matthew's eyes opened wider. "It looked a little more serious than that."

"To some people, dinner is a serious subject."

"But not to you. It never has been. You don't care so much about food."

Lily smiled, pleased that Matthew had taken the time to notice things about her. It made her feel better about herself that he liked her, even if Elijah didn't like her enough to change his plans. Elijah had chosen to upset her rather than upset the woman he barely knew.

Lily hadn't seen Elijah for a week, but she still couldn't get him out of her head. She had made herself busy with the project of sewing clothes for Tulip's *boppli* and then visiting Rose in between times.

Valerie had given Lily hope when she told her that God had a way of making things work out in miraculous ways. Lily clung onto that hope. She prayed every night that God might allow her another chance with Elijah. She decided the best course of action was to put her faith to work. If she made Elijah understand how she truly felt then he would marry her instead of that other woman. If he didn't, then it was possible that history would repeat itself and she'd become like Valerie and marry someone else while pining after the one man that she'd wanted.

Lily had never asked Valerie about Ed, but Lily had to wonder how hard Valerie had tried to persuade Ed not to marry someone else, or whether she'd been given any warning at all that he was going to marry another. One day, she'd find out the true story about Valerie and Ed, but today was the day to stop Elijah from thinking he couldn't go back on his word.

Lily prayed while she hitched the buggy and all the way to the Bontrager house, that all would go well when she was face-to-face with Elijah.

With a deep breath and one final prayer, she knocked on the front door. When it swung open, it was Elijah's brother, Jacob, who stood there. He looked similar to Elijah, but he was quieter.

She smiled, not wanting to let on how important this visit was to her. "Hi, Jacob. Is Elijah home yet?"

"Elijah's gone already."

Lily ran through her mind if there were any

community events on that night and couldn't think of a single one. "Where has he gone?"

"He left yesterday for Lowville. He's got some girl up there."

## *Chapter Seventeen*

Lily's mouth fell open and she couldn't hide her horror at what Jacob had just said. Forcing her mouth closed, she stared at him. "I see." She was too late! Either God had other plans for her, or He'd blocked His ears from her prayers. "I'll go, then." She turned briskly and, thinking the stairs were wider than they were, she stumbled down the two steps before managing to grasp the railing to steady herself.

Jacob stepped forward. "Are you okay, Lily?"

She swung to face him. "Fine! I'll see you 'round." Before she reached her buggy, she glanced over her shoulder at Jacob, who was still staring at her from the doorway. Feeling like a fool, she gave him a little wave before she jumped in the buggy.

Valerie, her new confidant, was the only person who would understand how she felt. She couldn't share this with her mother, and because she'd had a twin and two other sisters close in age, she had few close friends.

When she got to Valerie's house, she saw that she had visitors. She was sure it was Ed's buggy. Ed had a black horse with one white sock on one of his front legs. There couldn't be two horses the same as that in the community.

It seemed like Valerie's luck might finally be turning around, but what about Lily's? She had no choice but to keep traveling toward home. Then another thought occurred to her. She could talk to Rose and discuss things with her.

Lily was grateful when she stopped her buggy in front of Rose's house and there were no other buggies outside. That meant she had no visitors.

She opened the door just slightly. "Rose."

"Come up."

Lily closed the door behind her and hurried to Rose's bedroom. Rose was on the bed breastfeeding the baby. "Where's Mark?"

"He's just gone out to get a few things."

"Good. I wanted to talk to you alone."

"Anything wrong?"

Lily told her everything, leaving nothing out. "So, what's your advice?"

"That's hard."

"I know. That's why I need your advice. What would you do?"

"Nothing. *Gott* is watching over you and He'll find you the right man."

"So, you're saying Elijah isn't the right one."

"If he marries someone else he can't be."

Lily sighed. "I hate being in this situation." And what she hated more was that she couldn't talk to Daisy about it. Daisy and she would be able to figure the whole thing out. She didn't like Rose's idea of doing nothing. That seemed like madness. "Can I have a hold?" Lily asked when Rose finished feeding the baby.

"*Jah*, hold her upright so she'll burp."

Lily carefully took the baby from her sister and held her upright, and when Sarah gave a large burp, Lily giggled. "I want to have a little *boppli* like this one day."

"You will."

"I dunno."

"*Jah*, trust me."

"I have to find someone to marry."

"You've got so many young men interested in you."

"The one I want is off somewhere with someone else."

Rose said, "Pray about it."

Rose was quickly getting on Lily's nerves. Did Rose think she hadn't prayed about it already? Lily only stayed a few minutes longer.

* * *

The weeks passed and Lily had heard nothing of a marriage between Elijah and a woman from the community in Lowville. Neither had he thought to even write her a letter telling her he had to leave sooner than he'd first told her.

Each day, Lily had the same routine and while performing her chores, working at the flower stall and attending the community events, all she could think about was Elijah Bontrager. It hit her out of the blue one day that she hadn't heard about his marriage because he'd asked his family to keep quiet about it. He would've known she'd be upset about it and he was trying to save her from pain. Elijah was thoughtful like that.

In a further effort to put him out of her mind, she decided that she'd go out with the next man who asked her out, regardless of who that man was or what she thought about him.

It was a Tuesday afternoon after closing when Matthew and Lily were packing up their stalls that Matthew asked her if he could drive her home from the volleyball game that night.

"I don't know if that will work because I'll have to take the cousins home after the game."

"Why don't I bring you and the cousins to the volleyball game? Then I'll drop the cousins back home when it's finished, after which, you and I can go on a buggy ride. How does that sound?"

It wasn't ideal. Everyone would know she was going on a buggy ride with him. Her mother and father would know, and the cousins, Violet and Willow, would know as well. She had to say yes, since she remembered that she'd told herself she'd go on a date with the next man who asked. It was probably just as well that it was Matthew rather than someone totally unsuitable. Otherwise, she'd sit at home alone thinking about Elijah while he was creating a new life with another woman.

"Okay, Matthew, that sounds good."

"I'll collect you all at six thirty."

"We'll be ready."

Lily already felt a little better. Perhaps this is just what she needed—some male attention to make her forget Elijah.

Nancy noticed that Lily looked a little brighter as soon as she breezed into the kitchen. "Have you had a good day?"

"*Jah.* It was okay. Matthew is taking us to the volleyball game and then after we bring the cousins back here, I'm going on a buggy ride with him."

Nancy noticed that Lily seemed a little embarrassed to tell her the plans. "That's wonderful news."

"It's nothing to make a fuss over. It's not as

though we're getting married or anything like that. It's just a plain old buggy ride."

"I know that, but I haven't seen you look this happy for some time. I'm just pleased about it, that's all. I'm not planning the wedding already." Nancy chuckled while in her head she tried to stop herself doing just that.

"Well, I'm glad that me being happy is making you so pleased, *Mamm.*"

Nancy didn't know what it was with Lily, but there was some kind of disconnect between them and she never knew whether Lily was being sarcastic or not.

"Did you say someone was taking us to the volleyball game?" Violet asked as she and Willow walked into the kitchen.

Lily answered, "*Jah*, Matthew Schumacher."

"Are you in love with him?" Willow asked with a big smile on her chubby face.

Violet dug her sister in the ribs. "Lily doesn't like you talking about things like that."

"That's right. Someone might get the wrong idea," Lily said, frowning at Willow.

"But you are going on a buggy ride with him, right, Lily?"

"I am. But that doesn't mean I'm in love with him. That means I'm getting to know him a little better."

Willow sucked her cheeks in while she thought

about that for a moment. "But you already know him," said Willow.

"How about you two girls help me with the vegetables while Lily goes upstairs to get ready?"

Lily glanced over at her mother and smiled before she headed upstairs.

Just as Lily had closed her door, her mother burst in without knocking.

Glaring at her mother, she had her mouth open to speak when Nancy cut across her. "You really should give Matthew a chance."

"What do you mean?"

"I know you're going out with him later tonight, but I also know you've still got your heart set on Elijah. You should know that your *vadder's* heard some things about Elijah. It's right that he is getting married to a woman in Lowville."

"*Mamm*, that was never in doubt."

"You were hoping he'd change his mind."

"He hasn't, so I'm going out with Matthew just like you wanted."

"I want you to see Matthew for the good person he is without thinking constantly about Elijah."

"I'm trying to do that. It's not easy, but you should be pleased that I'm trying."

"It's not about me, it's about you."

"What would happen if I never married?"

Her mother gasped and covered her mouth. "You can't think like that."

"Would it be so bad?"

"You're only thinking that because of Elijah. I'm guessing you would've married him and you're only lonely now because Daisy has gone."

Lily slumped down onto her bed. "I can't help the way I feel. Don't worry about me, I'll be fine."

"I'll leave you alone to have a think about things."

Her mother said she was going to leave, but before she did, she kept droning on about how wonderful Matthew was and how good it would be if Lily married him because he was already her brother-in-law anyway. Lily was tempted to ask why it was so good to marry one's brother-in-law, but that would've kept her mother there longer.

"I'll give him a chance, *Mamm*."

Her mother smiled. "You will?"

Lily nodded. "But that doesn't mean we're going to get married. I'm going on one buggy ride with him and then we'll see what happens."

"That's all I can ask."

"I'm glad. Now, can I get ready please?"

Her mother, still smiling, stepped out of her room and closed the door.

Lily threw herself back heavily onto the bed. Staring up at the ceiling, she wondered what was to become of her. Daisy was gone and now life was hard instead of fun. She no longer wanted to stay in that house without her twin and getting married seemed the quickest way for her to be able to leave. Since she'd started her job she'd been saving as much as she could, but she figured it would take about ten years before she could get enough money for a deposit on a home of her own.

"I'm trapped and the only way out is marriage," she mumbled aloud.

Closing her eyes, she imagined what it would be like to be a married woman. She would be in charge of herself and wouldn't have to listen to anyone. That is if she married a man she could wrap around her little finger—a man such as Matthew. It would be good to have her own home and she would open the windows and the curtains. She wouldn't have it all closed up and dark like her mother's home. It would be full of joy and sunshine. She would have a beautiful, shiny black buggy horse like Ed Bontrager's, and she would call the horse Midnight. Her garden would be full of herbs and flowers and she'd keep fruit trees. Her husband would be tall and handsome and tell her how wonderful she was all the time and he'd compliment her cooking. The idea that she and Daisy had often talked about—having twins— still pleased her and that way she could have more children faster.

Lily felt better after visualizing her perfect life,

but now it was back to reality. And the reality was that tonight she would do what her mother said and give Matthew a chance.

## Chapter Eighteen

Later that night, Matthew was right on time when he collected Lily and the cousins. Violet and Willow hurried to the buggy first and got in the back and then Lily climbed into the seat next to Matthew.

"Are you ready to go?" he asked with a big smile on his face.

"*Jah*, you may leave now," one of the cousins said from the back with a giggle.

Lily made a good effort to keep Elijah out of her mind so she could concentrate on Matthew.

When they reached the park where the games were being held, the cousins jumped out of the buggy before it had come to a complete stop, and ran to meet their friends.

Matthew laughed. "They remind me of how you and Daisy used to be."

"Don't remind me of her."

When he had brought the buggy to a complete stop, he looked at her. "I'm sorry, you must be missing her."

"Just a little bit. Things will never be the same without her."

"They will, Lily. Just give things time." He jumped down and secured his horse.

Lily swallowed hard. Had time done Valerie any good when Ed had married someone else?

Matthew and Lily walked down the slight slope to join the others on the field.

"Are you going to play today?" Lily asked Matthew.

"I sure am."

Some of the men yelled out to Matthew to join their team when they saw him.

He turned toward Lily. "Are you going to watch me?"

"I will. You go ahead. It looks like they're waiting for you."

Matthew hurried toward his friends to make up the numbers in the team.

Lily looked around for Violet and Willow. Once she saw where they were, she sat down on one of the benches in the grandstand. Tonight, the cousins were her responsibility.

While she watched Matthew play, she realized he was good at everything. Everyone liked him, and she couldn't find one flaw in him. Her mind drifted to Elijah. In a way, it was a blessing that he was living far away. It would be painful to see him married to someone else and living in the same community. In time, she might not even think about him at all.

She noticed someone walking over to her. It was Nathanial, Matthew's cousin. It was odd that they were cousins and yet they were so different. He sat down next to her without being asked.

"Matthew tells me you're going on a buggy ride with him tonight, Lily."

"That's correct." She stared at him, knowing he was going to make some snide remark about his cousin.

"You shouldn't lead him on, you know. He'll only get hurt when you end up choosing me."

Maybe he was joking, but Lily was in no mood for jokes or small talk. "That's where you're wrong because I'm not gonna choose you."

He gave an exaggerated gasp and put his large hand over his heart. "You're killing me."

When he pulled a funny face, she couldn't help but laugh.

"Stop it. I'm going on a buggy ride with Matthew and there's nothing you can do about it."

He shook his head. "I thought you were more sensible than that."

"Where did you get the idea that I was ever

sensible? Anyway, I gave you a chance once and that's all you deserve."

He laughed.

She ignored him and kept watching Matthew, although she could feel that Nathanial was still staring at her. He needed to be put firmly in his place. "Matthew's quite handsome, don't you think?"

"*Jah*, very."

That wasn't the response she was expecting. "You really think so?"

"Of course. It runs in the family genes."

She shook her head. He always had a quick answer. "You would say that."

"Only because it's true."

Taking her eyes off Matthew and his game for a moment, she stared at Nathanial. "Are you saying that you're handsome?"

His mouth gaped open. "I would never say anything like that. You just said it."

"*Nee*, I didn't. Clean out your ears. I said Matthew was."

"Same thing. You think my cousin's handsome, then you must think that I am because I'm much better looking."

"It seems as though you are trying to ruin your cousin's buggy ride with me. Don't you have any shame?"

*"Nee."* He leaned closer. "And I never stop until I get what I want."

"You're dreadful."

*"Denke.* I'll take that as a compliment. Better to have some reaction from you than no reaction at all."

Lily shook her head at him, but she couldn't help smiling. It was never boring to be around Nathanial. And she hated to be bored.

"You should leave a message with your cousins for Matthew, that you've gone home with me, or rather, that I have taken you home. You could say you don't feel well."

"Ah, that would be a lie, though, because I feel fine."

"You're missing the point, Lily. We could get out of here right now and go somewhere exciting. I only came so I could see you. At least come and have a drink with me somewhere."

She gave a laugh and for a split second his idea was appealing until Matthew approached them wiping his face with a towel.

"You weren't watching me, Lily," Matthew said.

"I was watching you most of the time until your cousin deliberately distracted me."

Matthew threw his towel over Nathanial's face. "The best thing you can do with Nathanial is to ignore him."

Nathanial grabbed the towel and flicked it back at Matthew, who managed to duck out of the way.

Lily giggled at their clowning around.

Matthew took the towel back and sat down on the other side of Lily. "I apologize for my cousin if he's been harassing you."

"That's not very nice, cuz." 'Cuz,' short for cousin, was what they called each other.

Matthew laughed, leaned over and flicked the towel at Nathanial behind Lily's back.

"Ow, that got me."

"It was supposed to," Matthew said, laughing. "I hope he's not trying to stop you going out with me later tonight."

"*Jah*, he was. He said I'd have more fun going with him."

Matthew frowned at Nathanial.

Nathanial said, "I told Lily she should give a real man a chance."

Matthew looked around about him. "Where is this real man that you speak of? I can't see him anywhere."

Nathanial stretched out his arms. "I'm right here."

"I'm going on that buggy ride with Matthew." Lily made the statement while looking straight ahead.

"*Denke*, Lily. You heard it straight from Lily's lips, Nathanial. Sorry to disappoint you."

Nathanial sighed. "You can't blame a man for trying." He stood up. "Well, I'll leave the two of you by yourselves and see if I can't squeeze into one of the teams."

"You do that, cuz," Matthew agreed.

When Nathanial walked away, Matthew leaned in close to Lily. "I'm sorry about that, Lily. He has trouble knowing when he's overstepping the line. Feel free to tell him to leave you alone next time, or come and get me."

"I didn't want to be rude."

"You wouldn't be with people like Nathanial. That's what they understand."

"Are you going to play another game?"

"I might, but there are enough people here so I can sit down for a while."

Lily looked back at the games. There were four nets set up. Three games were ongoing and Nathanial was now amongst the last group sorting themselves into two teams.

"You should have a game, Lily." He nodded over toward where the teams were playing.

"I'm not very coordinated. It would be a disaster."

Matthew chuckled. "It would be fun to watch."

Lily pouted. "You're supposed to be on my side."

"I'll always be on your side." Matthew moved closer to her until their shoulders touched.

Lily looked over at the field again. "Look, Willow's having a game."

"That's not a good idea because of her sore shoulder."

"She says she's better. Do you think I should stop her?"

"*Nee*, let her play and have some fun."

Lily nodded. "Okay."

"It's not a serious game, so I don't think she'll get knocked down."

"I hope not, otherwise I'll be in trouble from Aunt Nerida. And she might never talk to *Mamm* again."

"I don't think there's a chance of that happening."

Lily didn't say anything to him but he should've been aware that Nerida and her mother hadn't been close for years. They would only speak to each other when they had to.

Lily and Matthew sat there the whole game and watched Willow. It was the same game that Nathanial was playing in but they were on different teams.

"She's playing quite well for someone of her build and with a sore shoulder."

"I didn't know she could play that well."

## Chapter Nineteen

The cousins had been taken back to Lily's home and now Lily's date with Matthew had begun.

She was nervous as the horse traveled back down their narrow dirt-packed driveway. She didn't know why she was so nervous because she saw him every day. Was it a mistake agreeing to go out with him? If things went wrong, she'd still have to see him every day at the markets.

A part of her wanted him to turn around now and she'd explain that they could only ever be friends, but her mother's words about giving him a chance rang in her ears. Perhaps after tonight, she might feel differently toward him.

"Do you know where we're going?"

He looked over at her and laughed. "No, not really. I just figured we'd see where the night took us."

"It looks like the night's taking us near the Glicks' farm."

"I thought I'd take you around some of the old winding roads out the back of their property. Unless you'd like to head into town where there are bright lights. We could go and have a cup of coffee somewhere."

"No, let's see how these roads look at night. I like driving at night."

He looked over at her. "Do you?"

"*Jah*, I like the fresh cool air and... I don't know. It's kind of exciting."

Matthew laughed at her. "You always look for the fun in things."

"I used to, but now Daisy has gone things are different."

"You've become sad, have you?"

She looked at Matthew's smiling face and knew he wouldn't understand what it was like having the person you've lived with every day for over twenty years suddenly being taken from you. "Things are different now."

"I know. I know it must be hard for you to be without Daisy."

"I don't know that anyone can understand it without being a twin themselves. We're identical twins, which means we're nearly the same person. We're two halves of a whole." Lily just hoped that Daisy remembered that—wherever she was.

Keeping his eyes on the road, Matthew rubbed his chin. "Something tells me your mind is elsewhere tonight."

"*Nee*, it's not."

He gave her a quick look. "Do you want to do this another night?"

She did, but what would her mother say if she got back to the house so early? "I'm okay."

"Let's do it another night when you feel like it. I honestly don't think that tonight's the right time."

"Okay. We'll do this another night. I guess I'm feeling out of sorts and in a strange mood. I'm sorry, Matthew."

He slowed down, and then turned the buggy around. "Don't worry about it. It's best that we leave this for another time."

"*Denke*, Matthew." She sat in uncomfortable silence as the horse trotted back to her house.

When he stopped the buggy at her house, things were even more awkward.

"Here we are," he said.

"Would you like to come in for a cup of hot chocolate? I know *Mamm* and *Dat* would like it if you did."

He smiled at her. "And you?"

"*Jah*, of course I would like it. I didn't mean that they were the only ones who would want you to come inside."

He shook his head. "*Nee*, Lily. You go and have an early night. I'll see you tomorrow."

"Okay." She jumped down from the buggy and headed to her house while he turned his buggy around. Once she got to the door, she waved to him as his horse walked down the driveway.

When Lily walked inside, she was pleased that her mother wasn't waiting there to find out what had happened. All Lily wanted to do was get into bed. She had hoped that spending time with another man would take her mind off Elijah, but it hadn't worked. If anything, it had brought home how much she and Elijah were suited. It had been a mistake to go on a buggy ride with Matthew and she hoped it hadn't ruined their friendship.

Lily was shaken awake the next morning. She looked at her mother through half-opened eyes. "Why are you waking me so early?"

"It's not early. It's time to wake up. If you don't wake up now, you'll be late for work and you know how Mrs. Walker hates it when you're late."

She sat up in bed. "I'm awake."

Her mother laughed. "Only just."

"I don't want to be late."

"How did things go with Matthew last night?"

And there it was. The question that Lily knew she would have to answer sooner or later. "I won't be going out with him again. Anyway, we see each other every day at work. We really had nothing to talk about."

Her mother leaned over and kissed her forehead. "You'll figure things out."

"I hope so." She didn't talk about Elijah. Her mother wouldn't understand.

As Lily got ready for work, she knew she could never marry someone unless she was in love with them—and just as much in love with them as she'd been in love with Elijah.

Besides, how would it be fair on the man she married if she wasn't really in love with him? Everyone deserved to have someone who loved them. She shook her head in an effort to get rid of the images of Elijah that kept jumping into her mind.

## Chapter Twenty

Lily arrived at work feeling awkward about seeing Matthew after their disastrous buggy ride the night before. At least she had explored the idea that they might make a good match. Her mother had to be grateful for that.

Throughout the day, Matthew was polite but he kept his distance. Neither of them mentioned the night before. Matthew had to know that things were never going to work out between them.

When she was getting into her buggy to go home that afternoon, she saw Nathanial jogging toward her.

"Wait up," he called out, waving her down.

She got out of her buggy to see what he wanted.

"How did your buggy ride go with Matthew?"

"Didn't your cousin tell you?"

"We don't talk about everything."

"That's good to know."

"If you haven't made any long-term commitments to him, I would like you to come out with me," Nathanial said.

"We already did that, remember?"

"That was some time ago. Come on, just give me another chance."

"Why, have you changed?"

"I'm always changing and growing and becoming a better person."

When she stopped and stared at him, she could see that he wasn't joking. To make that comment he had to have known he needed changing. She seriously considered another date with him. Things with Matthew hadn't worked out so what better things did she have to do with Elijah gone?

"Maybe I will, but it won't be any time soon."

"What about this Saturday afternoon? I'm working in the morning but I could swing past your place after that and then we could go somewhere."

Lily shook her head. "I don't know."

"What's to stop you?"

She bit her lip. "Nothing, I guess."

"It's done then." He clapped his hands, causing her to jump with fright. "I'll collect you after work on Saturday. I can't give you an exact time. It'll be sometime between twelve and one." He turned around to walk away.

"I haven't said that I will go with you," she called after him.

"I won't take no for an answer. And if I have to come in and speak to your parents and tell them how I've changed, I will."

"I don't think that will be necessary." Lily remembered that her parents were taking the cousins back to Nerida's on Saturday.

"I'll see you then."

Somehow, Nathanial always managed to make Lily laugh. She liked his bright and breezy carefree manner, whereas Matthew was quieter and although he was funny sometimes, he was generally serious-minded. But was Nathanial a man she could trust? He'd always treated her respectfully and politely and that was why she'd begun to doubt what Daisy had said about him.

If Matthew had deserved a chance, it seemed only fair to give Nathanial one. After all, she'd liked him before Elijah had come along. She only hoped Matthew wouldn't be upset that she had agreed to go out with Nathanial.

The time eventually came when Nerida had recovered enough to have her daughters at home.

"Are you sure you don't want to come with us when I take the girls back home, Lily?" Nancy asked.

"*Nee*, you go. I'll stay home and do a few things. I might go out a bit later on myself."

"Okay. We'll be gone for a few hours."

Nancy wondered why her daughter seemed so keen to stay home alone. Perhaps she was upset and would feel better when she'd had time to think things through.

Nancy got the two cousins organized with a bag of clothes and they all piled into the buggy that Hezekiah had just readied and had waiting for them by the front door.

"Are you going to miss us, Aunt Nancy?" Willow asked.

"Of course we are going to miss you. You've both been so good. You can come back and stay at any time."

"Will you tell *Mamm* we've been really good?" Willow asked.

Hezekiah chuckled. "We'll be certain to do that, but I don't think your mother would be concerned that you weren't on your best behavior."

"We're not always good at home," Willow said.

"I think you're good enough," Nancy said, thinking of how dreadful the twins could be sometimes.

Nerida's place was close, only fifteen minutes by buggy.

John opened the door when Nancy knocked at the front door of Nerida's house. Nancy was impressed that the two girls, Willow and Violet, stayed politely behind her rather than rushing past her like her daughters would've.

"Come in," John said with a big smile. He opened his arms to his daughters as Nancy walked past him. He gave his daughters a big hug. Once they were through the door, Hezekiah walked inside.

Nancy then followed John and the girls into the living room. Nerida was on the couch with her leg elevated.

"Can you get around yet, Nerida?"

She pointed to a cane on the other side of the room. "I've got a stick to help me walk, but it's still quite painful."

"I can keep the girls for longer if you want me to."

"*Nee*, they should be fine. They can help with things in the house."

"Now I can go back to work," John said with a laugh.

"He's been a good nurse."

"I did my best. I don't know that I'm cut out for it."

"We could've looked after you, *Mamm*," Violet said.

"Well, you can look after me now. I didn't want to burden either of you with all my pain."

John laughed. "But it was all right to burden me with that?"

Everyone laughed.

"Should I make us all a cup of tea?" Nancy asked.

"*Jah*, *denke*, Nancy. The girls will help you."

"They can stay here with you. I can make it by myself."

John looked at Hezekiah. "And while that's happening, I have something I want to show you in the barn."

"Let's go."

While the men went to the barn, the girls sat close to their mother while Nancy went into the kitchen. Nancy was pleased things had finally mended between herself and Nerida. Two years ago, Nerida would've never allowed the girls to stay with her, even in the same circumstances. To enable them to become friends again, Nancy had needed to let go of the notion that she had been right and Nerida had been wrong.

After Nancy had made the tea, she found a tray upon which to place the tea items and then she carried it out to the living room.

"I wonder what *Dat* is showing *Onkel* Hezekiah in the barn," Violet said.

Nerida laughed. "I'd say they're getting away from the women."

"*Jah*, that's what I thought, too," Nancy said.

After they talked and drank tea, Nerida suggested that the girls unpack their clothes.

Once they were gone, Nerida and Nancy were alone. Nancy knew she'd have to stick to neutral topics of conversation to avoid anything that would cause an argument.

"How does it feel to have all your daughters married now?"

"Well, I still have Lily."

"She's as good as married, isn't she? I heard she and Matthew might be getting married."

"Nothing but rumors." Nancy was relieved that there had been no rumors about Nathanial and Lily. "Lily had her eyes on someone and he liked her too, but now he's gone."

"I'm sorry to hear that. It must be upsetting for Lily."

"*Jah*, she is very upset about it. I don't think I'll have Lily off my hands for some time."

"It was so nice of you having Violet and Willow stay with you."

"I loved having them there. It'll be quiet now with just Lily."

"Enjoy the time you have with her since she's your last one now. I must say that I often envied you having six *kinner*."

Nancy was pleased that they were back to telling each other things. "You did?"

"*Jah.* The more *kinner* you have, the more *grosskin.*"

Nancy laughed. "I suppose that's true, but my *grosskin* haven't been quick in coming. I'm happy that Tulip is now expecting."

"*Jah*, me too."

"I do hope we can be closer, Nerida, like we once were."

"There is no reason why we can't be."

"It saddens me that we lost all those years."

"We shouldn't look back; we should only look forward."

"That's true. We'll move forward together." Nancy reached over and held out her hand. Nerida put a hand in hers.

"You know, it was all due to me that my girls married when they did," Nancy admitted with a giggle.

"It was?"

"*Jah.* I'll tell you about it sometime."

"I'd like to hear about it because I want Violet and Willow to marry young."

The girls appeared in the living room.

Nancy leaned over and whispered, "I'll tell you all my secrets another time."

"Good!" Nerida said with her face now lit up. "I'm looking forward to it. You and I might be able to devise some plans to speed up the process."

## Chapter Twenty-One

While her mother was taking the cousins back to Nerida's, Lily got ready for the buggy ride with Nathanial. She guessed that her mother and father would be gone for most of the day and if she planned things just right, she could be back before they got home. She might never even have to tell them about it. She doubted that she'd ever continue a relationship with Nathanial, but for now, he was a good distraction to take her mind off the man she really wanted to be with.

Nathanial jumped down from the buggy and walked toward the house. Lily hurried out to meet him.

"Hi. Where are Hezekiah and Nancy?"

"I think that's Mr. Yoder and Mrs. Yoder to you, Nathanial."

Nathanial laughed.

"Aren't they home? Remember that I said I was going to come by and make sure it was all right for us to see each other today?"

"I told you there's no need for that. They're out now anyway."

"Well, come on." Nathanial took his hat off and ran a hand through his dark hair. "Are you all ready?"

"*Jah*, I'm ready to go."

"Well, let's go then," he said. Lily hurried to the buggy. "Are you in a rush to be alone with me?"

She shot her head back to look at him. "It was you who talked me into this, remember? We don't have to go at all. I don't mind."

"Calm down. I was just joking. You're certainly not the fun girl I remember from months ago," Nathanial said as he jumped in the buggy beside her.

Lily knew he was right. She'd enjoyed herself more and had been a happier person when Daisy had been around. Daisy was gone and nothing was fun without her, and worse than that, now Elijah was gone too. She had to make the best of things with Nathanial and maybe he could help her get out of the bad mood that she couldn't shake.

He turned the buggy around and trotted his horse down the driveway at a speed that would've horrified her mother, who always insisted that everyone walk the buggy on the driveway.

Nathanial glanced up at the sky. "Did you notice those storm clouds gathering?"

"*Nee*, I didn't. Do you think we should cancel the buggy ride? It's not gonna be much fun in the rain."

"I love the rain," Nathanial said with a huge smile.

"I normally like the rain and I love running in it, but only when I'm in the mood. Today, I'm not in the mood for it."

"The rain is good; we couldn't do without it. It gives our crops water, waters our animals and the birds, and the flowers need water too."

She looked at Nathanial. It seemed a strange thing for him to say. Was this a new Nathanial, or was he repeating what he'd heard someone else say?

"So is this going to be a fun buggy ride?"

He stared at her and raised an eyebrow. "You're putting me under a lot of pressure."

"You're always saying I need more fun. I thought this was gonna be a fun buggy ride."

"Give me a chance; it's only just started."

Lily giggled, finding amusement in seeing Nathanial squirm.

"We could go down by the river to the shops where I met you—when I ran into you with…oh, sorry, that was Daisy."

That was the last name she wanted to hear. How

could she forget Daisy when everyone kept saying her name? She shook her head. "Are you saying that you like Daisy more than me?"

"*Nee*, it's not like that."

"You don't see much difference between us? We're quite different you know."

"Why are you asking me these questions?" He slowed the horse as he looked over at her.

She shrugged her shoulders. "Why would I go for a buggy ride with you? I wouldn't if I knew you were still pining after my twin *schweschder*."

"You're more fun. I haven't thought about Daisy in ages."

"*Gut*, because she's married."

"I know that," he said.

"Anyway, I don't want to talk about Daisy."

"Neither do I."

"You're the one who brought up her name."

"I didn't mean to. We won't talk about the subject again."

Lily frowned. "There is no subject."

"It's a bit hypocritical of you to get angry with me for once liking Daisy."

"Why do you say that?"

He leaned closer to her. "I think you're in love with someone and you're pining after him."

"Don't be ridiculous, Nathanial."

"I know I'm right. You're different with me from how you used to be."

"You mean I'm no fun anymore?"

"I think you're in love with Elijah Bontrager."

Lily had nothing to say to that. She didn't owe Nathanial any explanation and neither had he any right to know anything about her life.

When she remained silent, he said, "I'm right."

"I don't want to talk about it. Now, where is this fun that you promised me?"

He pulled the horse over to the side of the road, and then stopped.

"What are you doing?"

He looked behind, and then turned the horse around. Once the horse was trotting back the way they'd just come, he said, "I'm taking you home."

"Why? You made such a fuss that you wanted me to go on a buggy ride with you and when I agree you take me home? You're mad!"

"You're no good to me if you're in love with someone else."

Lily looked down to her hands on her lap. "He left to marry someone else."

"Then you should tell him how you feel."

"How do you know I didn't?" she shot back.

"Because he's not here."

Lily shook her head. "There's more to it. It's a long story and it's not mine to tell."

"Is there anything I can do, Lily?"

"*Jah*, there is. Let's just go out to a cafe and get

something to eat. I really don't want to be alone right now. I just need a friend."

Nathanial smiled as he pulled the buggy to a stop, and turned it around again.

"My poor horse is most likely totally confused now. I can't leave a lady in distress. I'll be your friend for the next few hours." He leaned closer to her. "Don't let it get around that I'm a softie."

"*Denke*, Nathanial. I don't believe all those things people say about you."

He raised his eyebrows. "I guess that's a good thing."

Lily giggled and was pleased that she had a friend, even if it was only for the next few hours.

## Chapter Twenty-Two

At the next Sunday meeting, Lily's heart stopped when she saw him, and he didn't even look over at her. Lily looked around the crowd to see if Elijah had brought his new wife with him to the meeting. Amongst all the women, she couldn't see one woman she didn't know.

*Maybe his wife doesn't feel good after the long journey and is having a rest at home.*

Lily hoped that Elijah and his wife wouldn't come to live in Lancaster County. The only good thing about Elijah marrying someone else was that they would be living far away and she wouldn't have to see them all the time.

The meeting carried on and Lily hadn't heard one word of it even though her father was the one delivering the sermon.

As soon as the meeting ended and everyone

else made their way out of the house, Lily hurried over to Elijah. She'd convinced herself there was a glimmer of hope. Since she'd heard nothing about a marriage and there was no woman there, could he have changed his mind and not gotten married? Surely Valerie would've heard some whisper and told her if she'd heard Elijah was married. Besides that, there had been no announcement during the service that Elijah was back and had married.

It was odd that he hadn't looked around for her as everyone had filed out of the house into the yard. She walked over and tapped Elijah on the shoulder while he was pouring out a glass of juice for himself at the drinks table.

He turned around, but there was no hint of a smile in his eyes. "Hello, Lily."

She was concerned that he was so cold. Immediately, she knew that something was wrong. "Where have you been?"

"I went to Lowville to see Patricia."

The words cut her like a knife. She blurted out a question that she had to know the answer to. "Are you married?"

"*Nee.* I went there to explain the situation to her."

It was supposed to be good news, but the look on his face told her otherwise. Had his feelings toward her changed while he was gone?

Hoping 'the situation' meant that he'd explained

to Patricia he couldn't marry her because he was in love with Lily, she held her breath and waited for him to continue.

"I went there to tell her I couldn't marry her because I was in love with you."

The words were the ones she'd hoped to hear, but why was his face so stern?

"That's good, but you look like you're angry with me."

"I am. I probably just made the biggest mistake of my life."

"What do you mean?"

He frowned. "I get back here to find out in the short time I've been away, you've dated Matthew Schumacher and Nathanial. Nathanial, of all people."

Her heart sank into the bottom of her boots. She'd made a huge mistake by having anything to do with Nathanial. "I can explain all that. Anyway, why didn't you tell me what you were doing? I thought you'd gone away to get married. You didn't say anything to me and I've been so worried this whole time. You could've written to me or left me a note."

"Perhaps I should've married her. She didn't date anyone."

Now Lily was annoyed at his double standards. "Well, you dated someone else. You dated me. You hold me to a higher standard, but think it's okay for you to date me when you knew you'd promised to marry someone else." Lily pressed her lips together. She hated it when things weren't fair. "And you gave me roses."

"I can't be the least bit important to you if the very minute I'm gone, you jump feet first into dating other men as if I'd never even existed." He turned his back on her and finished filling his glass.

She held her stomach. Taking a step to stand by his side, she continued, "You don't understand. I love you so much and it feels so good to be with you and I thought I'd lost you. I was just trying to recapture how I feel with you, with someone else. But it didn't work."

Elijah turned to face her with his glass of juice in one hand. "Lily, save your words." And with that, he strode away.

She stood there staring after him. It wasn't fair. He wasn't being fair. What she'd done might seem bad to him, but why wasn't he looking at her side of things? Every day she'd thought about nothing but him. He might as well have married that other woman.

That same afternoon, Lily visited Valerie. Valerie was one of the few people with whom she could talk things over.

"Do you understand why I went out with those

two? I was just trying to recapture what I had with Elijah. I thought he was gone for good. I had to make myself forget him somehow, some way."

"*Jah*, I can see what you mean, but I can also understand how Elijah sees things."

"Does this mean I've lost him, Valerie? Tell me what you think."

"It's hard to say. Once you've lost someone's trust, it's hard to gain it back."

She sat there staring at Valerie, knowing that she was right. People had immediately believed bad things about Nathanial without finding out what he had to say. No one trusted Nathanial now.

"What can I do?"

Valerie shook her head. "You've explained yourself to him and I don't think there's anything else that you can do except wait."

"I've never been very good at waiting. Wait for what, anyway?"

"I think this is something that Elijah will need time to think over. He obviously loves you or he wouldn't have been so upset. In time, he'll see that you do love him and only him."

"I don't know. I think I've lost him all together. It was my *mudder's* fault. She was the one who told me I should give Matthew a chance."

Valerie laughed. "I don't think you can blame anyone. When you're an adult, which you are now, you're responsible for your own decisions no matter what. Did you have to take your *Mamm's* advice?"

"I guess not."

"You have to take responsibility for making the decisions that you've made, no matter who talked you into them."

Lily sighed. "It all seems so unfair."

"That's one of the things about life, it's not always fair. Blaming someone else and not taking responsibility is what's unfair."

"I guess I see what you mean. Even though *Mamm* told me she thought I should date Matthew, I was the one who agreed. I should've thought about it for myself. And as you said, the choice was mine."

Valerie nodded.

"I always thought I should listen to my parents."

"You're an adult now, Lily. You have to weigh things up. Even though you have to obey them about other matters since you're living under their roof, matters of the heart are different. Oh dear, I don't know if I'm making sense."

"You are. You're making perfect sense. It seems my *mudder* wanted to match me to someone and she likes Matthew."

"You could have her talk to Elijah and explain things to him."

"I couldn't do that. I don't think my *mudder* even knows how much I like him."

"You should talk with her the way you do with me."

Lily shook her head. "She sees me as someone else. You see me how I am, but… I don't know. I think my mother always thinks the worst of me. I've talked to her enough for her to know I like him, but I can't tell her more than that. You're far easier to talk to."

"You should try to talk with her."

"I find you much easier to have a conversation with. You don't judge me."

"I'm just trying to be of help. Maybe your *mudder* is trying to do that too in her own way."

"Anyway, whether I do or don't talk with her, it still doesn't solve my problems with Elijah."

"Pray about the situation and see what happens."

"I will. I just hope I haven't ruined the rest of my life. What if he goes back and marries her? It must've taken a lot for him to go back on his word. He did it for me. I know I'm going over the same things all the time, but no one else understands me and I don't have Daisy anymore. My cousins have gone home now too, not that I could've talked with them about Elijah. It's quiet without them in the *haus*."

"It would be. I got a letter from Bruno yesterday. They don't know when they'll be back. He said Daisy's starting to like it there."

Lily didn't like the sound of that. This had been Bruno's plan all along, to pretend he'd move to Lancaster County when all the time he was always going to take Daisy back to Ohio and stay there where his business was.

"I should go home. *Denke* for the tea."

"Come here anytime. I enjoy our conversations."

Lily giggled. "I'm glad you said that. I thought I was starting to annoy you."

Valerie laughed. "I know what it's like to be without the man you love. I know the circumstances aren't the same, but it's no more easy for either of us."

When Lily was driving away in the buggy, she remembered what Valerie had said. At least Valerie had lived with her husband for many years and had had that time with him. Lily had had no time with Elijah—not as husband and wife. Or perhaps Valerie had been talking about Ed Bontrager?

Lily was tempted to take up Daisy's invitation to visit her in Ohio. Remembering that there would be no one to look after the flower stall, she knew she'd have to stay put. On the way home from Valerie's house, she came upon Tulip and Wilhem's *haus*. Maybe another perspective would clear her head.

"Don't you see, Tulip? I won't feel the same way about any other man. Why did *Gott* want me to meet Elijah and then have it not work out between us?"

Tulip brought her fingertips up to her mouth as she yawned. "I don't know the answer to that, Lily. Have you heard that he's married the woman in Lowville yet?"

"*Nee*. You're not listening, Tulip. He told her he couldn't marry her and he's in love with me, but he came back and heard I'd been out with Nathanial and Matthew. He was upset with me."

"For what reason?"

"I didn't wait for him, but how did I know he'd be coming back? He told me he had to marry someone else, so what was I to do? Stay an old maid? Never marry while he goes off and marries someone else and has a brood of kids?"

"That doesn't make any sense. You'd find out eventually."

Lily frowned at Tulip. She wasn't listening at all. If she had been, her answers would've made more sense. "Are you concentrating on what I'm saying, or are you thinking about something else?"

Tulip rubbed the side of her head. "I'm listening."

When Lily was satisfied she had Tulip's attention, she continued, "I was trying to forget him and that's the only reason I went out with the others. He didn't listen to me and just walked away."

"What you should do is find out what's going

on in his head." Tulip yawned again. "I'm sorry, this *boppli* is making me tired." She covered her belly with her hand.

"I can see that. Do you want me to leave you alone so you can get some sleep?"

"I can't do that because then I won't be able to sleep tonight."

Lily figured she better ask something about what was happening in Tulip's life so it wouldn't seem like she'd come there solely to talk about herself. "So, what's it like having a *boppli* in your tummy?"

Tulip put her fingertips over her mouth and giggled.

"What's so funny?"

"It sounded funny the way you said it. Like someone came and placed a *boppli* in my tummy."

Lily pulled a face. "You know what I mean. What does it feel like to be pregnant?"

"Tiring. I haven't had any morning sickness at all, so I suppose that's something good, but I'm tired all the time."

"Have you been eating more than usual?"

Tulip took a moment to answer. "*Nee.* I don't think I have been. I guess I'll have to wait until the *boppli* grows bigger, then I might get more hungry."

Lily stayed a while longer and heard how Tulip was doing in her new marriage with Wilhem. It made Lily want to marry Elijah all the more. Tulip had been no help. She was far too vague and wasn't focused on what she was saying. Valerie had been the best person to go to.

## Chapter Twenty-Three

The following Sunday, there was no meeting as the services were held every second Sunday. Lily stayed in bed for as long as she could because there was no reason to get up.

Her mother opened the door. "Are you ever coming out of your room?"

"I guess so. What's the time?"

"It's just on midday and your *vadder* and I are going out to see Nerida, John and the girls. Would you like to come?"

Lily sat up in bed, pleased that she was going to have the house to herself. "*Nee*, but I'll get out of bed now." Sunday was Lily's favorite day because there were no chores on Sundays, except chores of feeding animals and collecting eggs. There was no cleaning or scrubbing and no washing of clothes. "I'll get up, but I'll stay here if that's all right."

"Of course. We'll be gone in about fifteen minutes."

"Okay. *Dat's* going with you and staying there the whole time you're visiting?"

"*Jah*, he's staying with me. He's just outside hitching the buggy. Did you want to see him about something?"

"*Nee denke.* Just asking."

Her mother left her alone and then just as she was getting dressed, she heard glass shattering. With her prayer *kapp* in her hands, she raced downstairs. Her mother was standing there with her hand on the front door handle.

"Oh, Lily, it appears we've had a little accident with one of the windows. *Dat* has just called the Bontragers and someone will be over to fix it soon." Her mother wasn't upset and her lips were tilted at the corners with a secretive smile. "You'll have to wait for one of the Bontrager boys. Bye." Her mother closed the door.

Her mother had to be helping her to be alone with Elijah so they could talk. Lily raced up the stairs and finished getting dressed. She changed out of her green dress into her grape-colored dress. Once she had her cape and apron on, she quickly braided her hair, fastening it to her head, and placed on her *kapp* before heading down to the kitchen for breakfast.

Lily poured the cereal into a bowl while giggling at the picture in her mind's eye of her mother breaking the window. That had to be the only answer since her mother wasn't the slightest bit upset over the broken glass and neither had she said how it had happened. Her parents were helping her and Elijah to reconcile.

Lily munched on cereal while she ran through everything she wanted to say to Elijah. This could be her very last chance of explaining everything to him. And she had to tell him exactly how she felt about him or she might regret it for the rest of her life.

It was half an hour later when she saw a buggy heading up the driveway toward the house. Looking closer, she saw it wasn't Elijah's buggy and she hoped that it might be one of the buggies the Bontragers used for work. Then she realized that they used a wagon to transport the glass.

She walked to the front door and opened it when she heard the buggy stop outside the house. It was then that she saw it wasn't Elijah; it was one of his younger brothers.

Jacob jumped down from the buggy. "How are you, Lily?"

"*Gut denke*. I thought Elijah might have come to fix the window."

He walked closer before he spoke. "He normally would have come here, but he didn't. I can tell you where he is right now if you like." With a quick raise of his eyebrows, he added, "He's alone."

"I'm not sure if he'll want to see me."

He smirked. "I think he would."

"Do you think so?"

Jacob nodded.

"Where is he?"

"He's at home repairing the roof. We got a leak in the roof with all that rain last night."

"*Denke*, Jacob."

"Are you going to see him?"

"*Jah*, I am."

"You better show me that broken window first. I'll have to take the measurements."

Once she took him around the other side of the house, he told her it would take him some time to measure the window and once he'd done that he would cut the glass to the correct size.

"I'll help you hitch the buggy if you'd like."

"*Denke*, Jacob. That'd be *wunderbaar. Dat* normally does it when he's around, but he's just gone out visiting."

"The sooner we get you on the road, the sooner you can go see my *bruder*."

She headed toward the barn, trying to keep up with his long strides.

When she got to Elijah's house, she saw him on the red roof of his white rendered home.

He looked around, saw her and then made his way down the ladder.

"Lily, I didn't expect to see you."

"Jacob told me where you were. I hope that's all right." When he stood there staring at her, she asked, "Can we talk?"

"*Jah*, we can sit on the porch."

Once they were seated, she began, "I wanted to explain to you how it came about that I went out with Nathanial and Matthew. You see, I was so upset about you…"

"You've already told me this, Lily. We spoke about this on Sunday after the meeting."

"But I need you to understand and see things from my point of view."

He shook his head. "You don't have to say anything. Both Matthew and Nathanial have come to me and explained that you were never interested in either of them."

"They did?"

He smiled. "*Jah*, they did."

"So does that mean you forgive me and things can go back to normal?" She held her breath, hoping that he would say that they could.

"I would've gone over to fix that glass myself but I thought you wouldn't forgive me for being so awful to you and not listening. I'm still a little mad at you for going out with them, but I can't be mad at you forever."

"I guess we both needed to see things from the other person's point of view. I had no idea why you'd gone to Lowville. Why didn't you tell me?"

"I wanted to surprise you."

Lily laughed. "Well, you did that, but not in a good way."

"I should've thought things through better before rushing off. I should've taken the time to tell you what I was doing. The problem was I didn't want to get your hopes up and have things not turn out the way you wanted." He reached out for her hand.

She gladly offered her hand to him and he held it tightly.

"I was fully prepared to marry her until I met you. Things are over between Patricia and I forever."

"How did the poor girl take the news?"

"Not too badly. It turns out that she'd fallen in love with a young Mennonite man. Her parents won't be happy, but she's now prepared to face that. Once I told her that I was going back on my word to marry her, it gave her the strength to tell her parents about the young man she liked."

Relief washed over Lily. "I'm so glad that this worked out well for everyone."

"It will work out, Lily, but only if you agree to marry me."

She smiled at him. "*Jah*, I do."

"Phew. I don't know what I would've done if you'd refused me."

"So Patricia had dated, or at least gotten to know a man, and you told me that she hadn't been seeing other men. That's what you told me last Sunday."

"I'm sorry. I was angry. I should've given you a chance to explain things. Will you forgive me?"

Lily normally would've joked with him but she didn't want to risk another misunderstanding with him. "I will. If you'll forgive me."

"I want to marry you, Lily, and as soon as we possibly can."

"That sounds *gut* to me."

"I'll have to work out where we'll live." He rubbed his chin. "At least I can stay on working for my *vadder* now that I'm staying here."

"It doesn't matter where we live. We could live with my parents until we save some money."

"We'll figure that out later. Now, are you certain you want to do this? There'll be no backing out." He stared into her eyes.

"I'm more than certain. You're not going to back out, are you?"

He laughed and shook his head. "Come on. Let's go and let your parents know."

Lily giggled. "You'll have to tell them."

"Okay."

## Chapter Twenty-Four

Nancy and her husband had not been home long when they saw that the window had been fixed and Lily was nowhere to be seen.

When Hezekiah came back in from the barn after tending to the horse, she told him, "It looks like my plan worked. Lily's left the *haus* and the window is fixed."

"I thought it was *our* plan."

"Maybe, but mostly mine since I was the one who broke the window. I had to hit it a lot harder than I thought I would have to."

Hezekiah laughed.

When they both heard a buggy, they headed to the living room and peeped out the window.

"What did I tell you?" Nancy asked. "Looks like things worked brilliantly. That's Elijah's buggy and Lily is sitting right beside him."

"I have to agree it seems promising," Hezekiah said.

"I'll go and put the pot on to boil for a cup of tea." Nancy raced to the kitchen, and was back just as Lily and Elijah walked through the door. "Hello, you two."

Lily looked from her father to her mother. "We've got some news to tell you."

"Okay, would you like to sit down in the living room, or perhaps in the kitchen?"

Nancy knew there was only one thing that they could have to tell her. They had sorted out their differences and were getting married. And it was about time.

"Let's sit in the living room," Elijah suggested.

Once they were all seated, Lily looked at Elijah, who was sitting next to her. "You tell them."

A smile spread across his face as he looked at Nancy and Hezekiah. "Lily has only just now agreed to marry me."

Nancy squealed with delight and both she and Hezekiah got out of their seats. Nancy kissed them both while Hezekiah kissed Lily and shook Elijah's hand.

"We haven't had a chance to talk to the bishop or anything. I suppose…"

"You could see the bishop today. You could go over there right now," Hezekiah said.

"There's plenty of time for that," Nancy said,

patting her husband on his shoulder. "First, I'll make us all a cup of tea."

Nancy headed to the kitchen, pleased that she had completed what she'd set out to do. Soon, she and Hezekiah would be alone to spend some years with just the two of them. It certainly would be quiet in the house without the girls. She wondered if she'd been too hasty pushing Lily to marry when recently she had expressed doubts about doing so, but what else would give Lily the happiness that a good marriage and children would give her?

Lily's mother brought the tea items out on a tray and set them down on the low table in front of the two couches. As she poured the tea, she asked Lily, "Have you told Daisy that you're getting married?"

"*Nee*, I wanted you and *Dat* to be the first to know and then we have to tell Elijah's *vadder*." Lily saw her mother's hands shaking a little. "I'll do that, *Mamm*." Lily took over pouring the tea into the cups.

"*Denke*." Nancy sat back onto the couch next to Hezekiah. "When will you tell Daisy?"

Hezekiah said, "I thought you'd want her to be the first to know."

Lily glanced at Elijah and then said to her mother, "You can tell her if you want."

"*Nee*, it's your news. You should tell her."

"Things are a bit funny between us now."

"You can't let things get between you. You've always had a special bond."

"Your *mudder's* right," Elijah said. "Daisy would appreciate hearing from you, especially now that you've got this special news—our special news."

She smiled at Elijah and wanted to do anything to please him. "Okay, I'll tell her after we tell your *vadder*, how's that?"

"That's perfect," Elijah said as he smiled at her.

Lily handed everyone a cup of tea. When she handed her father one she knew he was deep in thought about something. "What is it, *Dat*?"

"I'm thinking about you and Daisy, that's all."

"Can you concentrate on me for a moment? We're two separate people and I just want to be happy for myself for once without considering another person."

Her mother sipped her tea. "*Jah*, Lily, you should take this time to enjoy your happiness and not be so concerned for others like you usually are."

Her mother's words were sweet, but Lily knew her mother was being sarcastic. Lily thought her a little mean for having a jab at her on such an important night. Looking at Elijah, she hoped he didn't know that her mother didn't mean her words. Elijah caught Lily's eye and smiled at her with adoration in his eyes. He wanted a woman who was concerned for others, and if that's what he wanted then that's the kind of woman she'd become. She knew she had to grow up and be totally honest because that's the kind of woman Elijah deserved.

Lily cleared her throat. "I know you don't think I care for others, *Mamm*, but I will be more caring and considerate. I'm going to become a new person."

"I like the person you are now, Lily," Elijah said.

She smiled at her beloved. "I will be better—a new improved Lily."

Hezekiah chuckled. "Elijah, this is where you should say that she couldn't possibly improve."

Elijah laughed. "I'll learn these things over the years, I'd reckon."

Nancy turned to Hezekiah. "You're not trying to teach Elijah to be a sweet-talker, are you?"

"It's not sweet-talking if Elijah believes it. Or, if Lily thinks he believes it."

Nancy shook her head at her husband. "Don't listen to him when he's in a mood like this, Elijah."

"He's a deacon, so I must listen to him."

Everyone laughed.

"Well, that's true, I suppose," Nancy said before she turned to Lily. "I'm glad you said what you did just now, and I hope you mean it."

"I do. I've been immature, but the time has come for me to grow up and think of others and be an adult."

"I'll help you do that," Elijah said. "And you can help me do the same. We'll mature together."

"Okay." Lily was pleased that he was supporting her in front of her parents. He was the oldest son in the family and was already mature enough.

"Why not call Daisy now?" Elijah suggested.

"But we haven't told your *vadder* yet."

"That won't matter. He won't be offended."

Lily looked down into her hot tea and watched how the light reflected on the top of it in ripples. "I could call her. I've got the number for where she's staying. She might not be home."

"Do it now. I'll wait here and entertain your parents."

Lily looked into his sincere eyes. He gave her the strength to call Daisy. "Okay, I will." She sat there thinking about what she would say and how she would start the call.

"Well, what are you waiting for? The phone number of where she's staying is on top of the notebook in the barn."

"Okay." Lily rose to her feet, placed her tea and saucer on the coffee table, and headed out to the barn.

She grabbed the piece of paper with the phone number of Bruno's *onkel*, who they were staying with, picked up the receiver, and dialed the number. Bruno's *onkel* answered the phone and after a few pleasantries were exchanged, she asked if she could speak to Daisy. She was pleased when he said she was home and then with the receiver in her hand she paced back and forward as far as the phone's cord would allow. Then her heart froze when she heard the small voice on the other end of the line.

"Lily, is that you?"

"Daisy, yeah, it's me."

"Did you get my letter?"

"*Jah*, I did. *Denke* for sending it to me."

"How's the new *boppli*? I was surprised to hear about Tulip. She must be so happy. How are *Mamm* and *Dat*? Oh, and I heard about poor Willow and her sore shoulder."

Lily giggled and could barely stop.

"What's funny, Lily?"

Gradually Lily stopped laughing enough so that she could speak. "I've missed you. Things aren't the same without you here."

"I'll be back soon, so don't worry, and then things can go back to normal."

Lily didn't comment. Things would never be normal between them now Daisy had Bruno and now she had Elijah.

"Lily?"

"I'm still here. I'm calling to give you news."

"Good news I hope."

"*Jah*, it's about me."

"What is it?"

"Elijah and I are getting married."

There was silence and Lily held her breath, hoping Daisy would approve.

"Are you serious?"

"I am. We're in love with each other and we've never been so happy. He said he's never been as happy as this and neither have I. Now I know how you feel about Bruno." Daisy giggled. Lily had missed the sound of her twin's laughter. "I hope you come back soon."

"We will. We're coming back in about a week. Bruno wants to start fixing up the house and sorting out his work."

"That is a relief. I was scared he would try to make you stay in Ohio."

"I told him I didn't want to live in Ohio before we married."

"I know that, but I thought he might talk you into it."

"*Nee*, he didn't even try. When are you getting married?"

"I don't even know. No one else knows. We've only just now told *Mamm* and *Dat*. We still haven't even told Elijah's *vadder* yet. We're going to tell him this evening, and then I guess we'll go to see the bishop and work out a time for the wedding."

"Make sure you wait until I'm back."

"*Jah*, I will, but don't wait too long until you get here."

"I said we're coming back soon."

Lily sighed. "You said a week, so is it a week or is it soon?"

"I said about a week's time. It's tomorrow week, to be exact."

"Good, I'll look forward to it."

"I can't wait until I get back and hold my new baby niece."

Lily had to fight back tears and was feeling emotional. It didn't seem right that Daisy had been away when Rose's baby had been born. She should've been there. "If I have a *boppli*, you'll have to be there."

"I wouldn't be anywhere else. And you'll have to be in the room with me when I'm giving birth."

Lily giggled. "Okay, well you better not go back on it."

"I won't."

"If Bruno suddenly wants you to go to Ohio with him to visit all his relations again, you just tell him no."

"I definitely will. I'll tell him my twin comes first, especially when she's having a *boppli*."

"And that's exactly how it should be, *boppli* or not," Lily said.

"I'll be back home soon and I must go now and tell Bruno the good news."

"Don't go yet. I want to talk to you some more."

"We're in the middle of a meal."

"Oh, sorry."

"Call me back tomorrow afternoon. I'll be here and we can talk longer."

"Okay, I'll do that, but make sure you answer the phone. I feel awkward talking to Bruno's *onkel*. He scares me a little."

Daisy giggled. "He's really nice."

"I know." Lily remembered him from Daisy's wedding.

"Bye, Lily, and congratulations. Being married is so good."

"I'm looking forward to it. Bye, Daisy." Lily hung up the receiver and hurried back to her parents and Elijah.

When she sat down on the couch, her mother said, "That was a very long conversation."

"It wasn't that long, was it?" She looked at her father and Elijah and they both nodded. "Oh, sorry. Once I start talking, I can't stop."

"I'm glad you called her."

"Me too. I think things are back to how they used to be between us." She looked down at everybody's tea and saw that they had none left. "More tea?"

Her mother and father shook their heads, but Elijah said he would have another cup.

"I can scarcely believe that we're having another wedding so soon," her mother said. "Don't have it too soon, Lily. We've got a lot to organize and a lot of dresses to make."

"Daisy said she's coming back in a week, a week and a day, or something. She can help us do everything."

"I'm glad she's coming back. I was starting to worry."

"Me too." Lily handed a second cup of tea to Elijah.

"It'll be good to have her back," Hezekiah said. "Then they can make that *haus* they bought into a proper home."

"I was going to make curtains for them, but now I've got to sew for Lily's wedding."

"And that must take priority," Lily said, hoping she wasn't sounding too selfish. "I'm sure there'll be time for both."

Her father leaned forward. "What you said the first time was right. A wedding takes priority over everything else. This is an important time in your life. And I'm sure you both know the importance of the union."

"*Jah*, we do Mr. Yoder. I believe that we're both mature enough to accept the responsibility of marriage and everything that goes along with it."

Hezekiah nodded and sat upright once more.

"And where would you live?" Nancy asked.

"I've some money saved. We'll look around for a *haus*, or we might even build one."

"You can live here while it's being built," Hezekiah offered.

"*Denke*, that's kind of you," Elijah said.

Nancy's face beamed. "It's a large house. There are plenty of bedrooms."

"We'll see, *Mamm*, when the time comes closer."

"You've enough saved then?" Hezekiah asked Elijah.

Lily was a little embarrassed that her father had asked such a probing question. But then again, he was Elijah's future father-in-law.

"*Jah*, enough for a good deposit."

"That's impressive for a young man of your age."

"I've been working and saving for a long time. As soon as I finished school I started working for my *vadder*."

"One day he'll take over the business," Lily said.

When they had finished talking, Nancy and Hezekiah walked to Elijah's buggy with the happy young couple.

"I hope your *vadder* takes the news well," Lily said to Elijah as she climbed up into the buggy.

He chuckled. "Of course he will. He's very fond of you."

"Bye." Lily waved to her mother and father, and

Elijah gave them a small wave before he turned the buggy around.

Hezekiah and Nancy watched in silence side-by-side as the buggy disappeared.

Nancy tried to blink back her tears, but then she couldn't stop them. They streamed down her face.

"What's wrong?" Hezekiah put his arm around her shoulders.

"They've all grown up. I don't want them to grow up." She turned and buried her head into his comforting shoulder.

"Isn't this what you wanted? You wanted them all to get married, and now you've achieved that. You were the one who thought Elijah and she would make a good pair. You did a little bit of matchmaking and whatever you did worked. There's nothing to cry about."

His deep voice soothed her. "I know, but we had six and now we have none. I just remember back to how they were and I want to turn back the clock."

"Nancy, we've talked about this before." He turned her to face him. "We can't stop time, we can't turn back time, and we can't slow it down. That's why we need to appreciate every moment and thank *Gott* for every good thing that comes our way. Don't be sad that our *kinner* have grown up. Think of it this way, we were blessed with six *kinner*. Six! That's one more than five, and two more than four. It's even five more than one."

She couldn't help but giggle at him.

"How *wunderbaar* is *Gott* to bless us so greatly? And each of our six are so special and so different. And the six of those will all give us *grosskinner*. Soon, we'll have a house full of them."

"I know." She nodded and dabbed at her eyes. Then Hezekiah wiped away her tears with his fingers.

It was a weird thing she felt, and she'd tried to explain it to Hezekiah before and he didn't understand. Now that all her children were adults, she missed the people they were when they were children. Their funny little ways, their funny words for things, their giggles. When they were young, she longed for the time when she could sit down and have a conversation with them as adults, and now they were adults, she wanted to turn back time and spend time with them as children. It was a funny thing. She should've enjoyed the time with her children more when they were younger. Then again, isn't that what grandchildren were for?

"Better now?" Hezekiah asked.

"A little."

"Didn't you say you wanted to have time with me alone when all our *kinner* finally leave home?" he asked.

"*Jah*, but I never really thought that day would come."

"That day will soon be upon us," he said.

"They've all made good marriages. They're all happy and that's even more of a blessing."

Nancy nodded.

On the day Daisy and Bruno arrived home, Lily and Elijah were waiting for them outside their house.

Bruno and Daisy had taken a taxi from the bus stop. Daisy stepped out of the car and Lily and Daisy rushed at one another. Their bodies slapped together and they hugged tightly amidst giggles.

While they were occupied doing that, Elijah helped Bruno get the luggage out of the taxi.

"I hope you don't mind, but I used the spare key and I've got dinner in the oven for you," Lily said.

"You have?"

Lily nodded. "And I did some shopping for you, so you've got enough food for days without having to go out. I thought you'd be tired after your long trip."

"That's very thoughtful of you," Daisy said.

Lily was pleased with herself. She was trying to make a big effort to be more caring for people and be more like her mother.

The four of them went inside the house. The girls had their arms linked together while the men carried the bags.

After they had a bite to eat, Daisy insisted on

taking Lily around the property. The house was only small, but it was on a large lot.

The men stayed inside talking.

"I really missed you while you were away," Lily told Daisy. "Did you miss me?"

"Of course I did. That's a silly thing to ask."

"I know, but we had that big fight."

"Don't talk about it," Daisy said.

"So, you missed me even though you're married and Bruno is taking up all your time?"

"It's not the same thing. No one can replace you."

Lily was pleased to hear her say that. "Did he try to make you stay in Ohio?"

Daisy frowned. "*Nee*, not at all. I don't know why you keep talking about that. We bought this house and we wouldn't have done that if we were going to move to Ohio."

"Places can be sold or leased."

"Lily, you're so suspicious."

Lily pulled a face.

"I can't believe you're marrying Elijah."

"Why not?"

"It happened quickly. We didn't really even talk about it."

"Don't you like him?"

"I do. And I remember that you liked him, but I thought you liked Matthew as well."

Lily giggled. "I like him, but not like that. I

think that Rose wanted me to like him. She kept telling me how she had overlooked Mark and she thought that was the same thing with me and Matthew, but it was nothing alike."

"I can't wait to see Rose's *boppli*."

"You'll love her."

"I'm going there first thing tomorrow. Now, I've got something very important I want to say to you."

Lily gasped. "You're not pregnant already, are you?" Lily reached out a hand and touched Daisy on her stomach, and Daisy hit her hand away.

"Stop it! *Nee*, I'm not pregnant. Not that I know of, anyway. While we were coming back on the Greyhound, Bruno and I had an idea. I really hope you like it."

"What is it?"

"We were thinking that, if you want to, you and Elijah could build a house right next to us, right on this land. It's plenty big enough. It's large enough for us each to have horses, chickens, goats, pigs, and whatever we want."

"Really?"

*"Jah."*

"You mean it?"

Daisy giggled. "Do you like the idea?"

"I love it!"

"It'll be just like we always said—well, nearly. We wanted to live in one big *haus*."

"Correction. We wanted to marry twins and live in one big house."

Daisy nodded. "We didn't marry twins, but we can still live really close and see each other every day."

"I love that idea. Are you sure that Bruno doesn't mind?"

"He was the one who suggested it."

Lily giggled and wrapped her arms around Daisy. "I don't mind that you married him now."

"Everything will be good for both of us. We'll have *bopplis* at the same time—"

"Twins," Lily corrected her.

"*Ach, jah*, that's what I meant. We'll each have three sets of twins and we'll live side-by-side."

"Oh, I hope that Elijah agrees with the idea."

"If he doesn't, you'll simply have to talk him into it."

"I'll do my best."

"Bruno will be talking to him about it right now. I told him I'd take you for a walk and show you around and while I was doing that I'd tell you his idea. He said he'd talk to Elijah."

Lily took a deep breath and prayed to God and asked Him to find the right home for them, and she hoped that it would be right there next to Daisy and Bruno.

"And what do you think about Tulip having a *boppli*?"

"She's so happy. It took a long time. She didn't tell anybody because she didn't want to take the attention away from your wedding, but as soon as Rose's *boppli* was born she had to tell everybody."

"*Mamm* must be really excited."

"She is. And now she's looking forward to my wedding. You know what she's like, she loves organizing these things. She said that after my wedding she'll have no more *kinner* to plan weddings for."

"There's always Violet and Willow," Daisy said.

"*Jah*, she'd push Aunt Nerida out of the way and take over." Lily giggled. "Anyway, that'll be a few years away."

Daisy nodded. "I guess so."

"Let's go back to the *haus* and see if Bruno has said anything to Elijah yet. Elijah won't make up his mind right away. He takes a long time to think about things."

"He didn't take a long time to think about you."

"*Nee*, because at the end of the day, he's very sensible and he could see what a *wunderbaar fraa* I'd make him." Lily giggled while Daisy wrapped her arms around Lily once again.

"I've missed you, Lily."

"Me too."

They hurried back to the house. Lily was pleased to have a man who cared about her and loved her deeply, and she had her twin back.

\* \* \*

Weeks later, there was another wedding at the Yoders' *haus*.

Nancy hadn't expected things to happen so soon for Lily. Elijah was a decent hardworking man from a good family. Months ago, she'd secretly started hoping Lily might fall in love with him.

Nancy sat down, having a little rest from the cooking. Nerida had taken the reins for Lily's wedding and had done most of the organizing of the food, whereas in the past that had always been Nancy's job. Sitting next to Hezekiah, Nancy looked at her whole family and her grandchildren.

There was Tulip who was about to have her first child, sitting next to Wilhem.

Months before, Daisy and Bruno had bought a small house close to Nerida and John's farm, and were renovating it. Bruno had plans of adding on to it once the babies started arriving and she heard whispers of another house going up next to it. For now, though, Nancy was just pleased to have Daisy close to home rather than in Ohio.

"You've done a great job, Nancy," said Hezekiah.

"What do you mean?"

"All our *kinner* are now happily married. Each and every one."

She smiled at the appreciation on his face. "*Gott* helped bring the right people to them."

"Look how happy Lily is now. I haven't seen her like that in a long time."

Nancy looked over at Lily, who was sitting at the wedding table next to Elijah.

Nancy sighed. "They are so nice together—so well suited."

"I was worried about her there for a while. I know you don't like Nathanial, and I was concerned with what I was hearing back from people."

"I heard some things too, but we don't have to worry about that anymore."

"Don't we?" Hezekiah nodded his head and Nancy looked to see where he was directing her attention. It was Nathanial talking and laughing with Violet.

"He wouldn't dare! She's much too young for him."

"Not really. And Violet's getting close to marrying age."

"I'll have to warn Nerida about him."

Hezekiah smiled. "Haven't you done that already?"

She saw that her husband looked amused. "This isn't funny, Hezekiah."

"I think you should give him a chance," he said.

"To do what? Ruin some girl's life?"

"We've talked about this already and we both thought that Daisy might have exaggerated things."

"And if not—what then? Better to be safe than be sorry."

Hezekiah inhaled deeply. "The good thing is that at least you're getting along better with Nerida."

Nancy knew he was deliberately changing the subject. "We are, aren't we? It's been good to have her back in our lives. And you get along well with John too."

"I've never stopped talking to John."

"You know what I mean. It's good now that we can have them all over at the family dinners."

"We're getting more crowded for those dinners. We'll need a bigger *haus* soon."

"We'll just get an extra table in for the little ones to eat at. Like we had for our *kinner* when they were smaller."

Hezekiah nodded. "I've still got that table. It's in the barn."

"Clean it up and bring it inside."

"I will."

Nancy looked over at Tulip, who was looking most uncomfortable. She stood up and patted her husband on his shoulder. "I'll be right back."

Tulip smiled when she saw her mother approaching. "Hi, *Mamm*."

"How are you feeling?"

Tulip rested both hands on top of her swollen belly. "Fed up! I want this *boppli* out of here."

"Too early." Nancy giggled as she sat down next to her. Wilhem, who was sitting next to Tulip, started talking to people on the right side of him.

"There will be moments to come in the next few months when you realize how good it was right now."

"You mean all the sleepless nights?"

Nancy nodded. "I remember wanting my babies out and when I was tired or they wouldn't stop crying, I realized how lovely it was when they were in my tummy."

"I'll just be glad when they're out. I mean him, or her. *Ach, nee*, I didn't mean to make it sound like I'd have more than one. You don't think I'll ever have twins, do you? The nurse at the clinic said there's only one in there after she did the ultrasound."

"I guess you could have twins at some stage since it's supposed to run in families."

Tulip pulled a face. "I could cope with it. Daisy and Lily didn't turn out too bad."

"Eventually," Nancy commented. "Just try to relax and forget about things."

"Forgetting about being pregnant isn't easy to do. I can barely move and I feel like a stranded beetle most of the time."

Nancy wished she could help Tulip in some way. Tulip wasn't one to complain so Nancy knew she must've been feeling particularly down. She didn't know what other advice she could give her. "It's just what we women have to go through." Nancy bit her lip. Her mother had said that to her and it had annoyed her at the time.

Tulip sighed. "I guess it'll be worth it when I'm holding my *boppli* in my arms."

"That's right. It'll all be worth it. Just ask Rose."

While Tulip kept talking, Nancy looked around and at her grandchildren. They were all going to be growing up close together in age—just as she and Hezekiah had hoped they would be. She gave a sigh. With her last daughter now married, this would be the last wedding she'd hold at her house. She spied Ed Bontrager and Valerie talking close together. It had become a familiar sight to see them that way.

"Nancy!"

Nancy turned around to see a flushed-faced Nerida. "What's wrong?"

"Everything! We need your help in the kitchen."

As Nancy hurried back to the kitchen with Nerida, she asked, "What is it? Not enough desserts? Do you need more people to help with serving?"

Nerida pulled Nancy to one side. "*Nee*, Nancy.

I just didn't want to say anything in front of Tulip. Everything in the kitchen is fine."

"Oh!" Nancy had been secretly a little pleased to think that things weren't running as smoothly without her. "Well, what's wrong?"

"Nathanial Schumacher is talking to Violet. Look!"

Nancy didn't need to look; she'd already seen it for herself. "I know."

"What are we going to do? You said he was no good," Nerida said.

"That was some time ago and he could've changed."

"You only told me about him recently, and besides that I've heard other people say a few things."

Nancy looked over at the table where Nathanial and Violet were sitting. Now they were talking to others beside them.

"You see? They're not talking now."

Nerida sniffed. "I've only got the two *kinner*. It's more important for me to see that they marry *gut menner*."

Nancy frowned, trying to work out Nerida's logic.

Nerida continued, "I think we should find someone quickly for Violet before she is swayed by someone totally unsuitable."

"This young?"

Nerida nodded.

"She's not going on *rumspringa*?" Nancy asked.

"*Nee*, she doesn't want to. She's too nervous a girl for that. Your girls didn't go."

"They didn't want to either."

"Will you help me with this, Nancy?"

"Help you find a man for Violet?"

"*Jah!*"

"Who did you have in mind?"

Nancy and Nerida walked back toward the kitchen while discussing marriage prospects for Violet. Even though Nancy thought sixteen was far too young to be thinking of marriage, she was pleased that Nerida and she would be able to work on a project together.

Lily still couldn't believe how blessed she was to have married a man like Elijah. She also had her twin back in her life and they had found a way to be friends even though they both had men in their lives who kept them busy. Daisy had agreed to be Lily's wedding attendant and was sitting beside her at the wedding table. Surrounded by family, her nieces, her nephews, and her friends young and old, she knew she'd hold the memories of this special day in her heart forever.

Elijah and Bruno had been discussing plans to build side-by-side houses on the land where Bruno and Daisy were currently renovating their small house. It wasn't the same as living in one big house as Daisy and Lily had once dreamed, but they both agreed that it was close enough. The twins' dreams about their children growing up close by looked as though they were going to come true.

\* \* \* \* \*

*With her family in danger of being separated,
could marriage to a newcomer in town
keep them together for the holidays?*

*Read on for a sneak preview of*
An Amish Wife for Christmas *by Patricia Davids,
available in November 2018 from Love Inspired!*

"I've got trouble, Clarabelle."

The cow didn't answer her. Bethany pitched a forkful of hay to the family's placid brown-and-white Guernsey. "The bishop has decided to send Ivan to Bird-in-Hand to live with Onkel Harvey. It's not right. It's not fair. I can't bear the idea of sending my little brother away. We belong together."

Clarabelle munched a mouthful of hay as she regarded Bethany with soulful deep brown eyes.

"Advice is what I need, Clarabelle. The bishop said Ivan could stay if I had a husband. Someone to discipline and guide the boy. Any idea where I can get a husband before Christmas?"

"I doubt your cow has the answers you seek, but if she does I have a few questions for her about my own problems," a man said.

Bethany spun around. A stranger stood in the open barn door. He wore a black Amish hat pulled low on his forehead and a dark blue woolen coat with the collar turned up against the cold.

The mirth sparkling in his eyes sent a flush of heat to her cheeks. How humiliating. To be caught talking to a cow about matrimonial prospects made her look ridiculous.

She struggled to hide her embarrassment. "It's rude to eavesdrop on a private conversation."

"I'm not sure talking to a cow qualifies as a private conversation, but I am sorry to intrude."

He didn't look sorry. He looked like he was struggling not to laugh at her.

"I'm Michael Shetler."

She considered not giving him her name. The less he knew to repeat the better.

"I am Bethany Martin," she admitted, hoping she wasn't making a mistake.

"Nice to meet you, Bethany. Once I've had a rest I'll step outside if you want to finish your private conversation." He winked. One corner of his mouth twitched, revealing a dimple in his cheek.

"I'm glad I could supply you with some amusement today."

"It's been a long time since I've had something to smile about."

*Don't miss*
An Amish Wife for Christmas *by Patricia Davids,*
*available November 2018 wherever*
*Love Inspired® books and ebooks are sold.*

www.LoveInspired.com

# Love Inspired®

## Save $1.00

on the purchase of ANY

Love Inspired® book.

Available wherever books are sold, including most bookstores, supermarkets, drugstores and discount stores.

---

# Save **$1.00**

on the purchase of ANY Love Inspired® book.

Coupon valid until December 31, 2018.
Redeemable at participating retail outlets in the U.S. and Canada only.
Limit one coupon per customer.

**52616046**

**Canadian Retailers:** Harlequin Enterprises Limited will pay the face value of this coupon plus 10.25¢ if submitted by customer for this product only. Any other use constitutes fraud. Coupon is nonassignable. Void if taxed, prohibited or restricted by law. Consumer must pay any government taxes. Void if copied. Inmar Promotional Services ("IPS") customers submit coupons and proof of sales to Harlequin Enterprises Limited, P.O. Box 31000, Scarborough, ON M1R 0E7, Canada. Non-IPS retailer—for reimbursement submit coupons and proof of sales directly to Harlequin Enterprises Limited, Retail Marketing Department, 22 Adelaide St. West, 40th Floor, Toronto, Ontario M5H 4E3, Canada.

5 65373 00076 2 (8100)0 12392

**U.S. Retailers:** Harlequin Enterprises Limited will pay the face value of this coupon plus 8¢ if submitted by customer for this product only. Any other use constitutes fraud. Coupon is nonassignable. Void if taxed, prohibited or restricted by law. Consumer must pay any government taxes. Void if copied. For reimbursement submit coupons and proof of sales directly to Harlequin Enterprises, Ltd 482, NCH Marketing Services, P.O. Box 880001, El Paso, TX 88588-0001, U.S.A. Cash value 1/100 cents.

Looking for inspiration in tales
of hope, faith and heartfelt romance?

Check out **Love Inspired**® and
**Love Inspired**® **Suspense** books!

**New books available every month!**

---

**CONNECT WITH US AT:**

Facebook.com/groups/HarlequinConnection

 Facebook.com/HarlequinBooks

 Twitter.com/HarlequinBooks

 Instagram.com/HarlequinBooks

 Pinterest.com/HarlequinBooks

ReaderService.com

*Love Inspired*®

LIGENRE2018R2

## Inspirational Romance to Warm Your Heart and Soul

Join our social communities to connect with other readers who share your love!

Sign up for the Love Inspired newsletter at **www.LoveInspired.com** to be the first to find out about upcoming titles, special promotions and exclusive content.

### CONNECT WITH US AT:

Facebook.com/groups/HarlequinConnection

 Facebook.com/LoveInspiredBooks

 Twitter.com/LoveInspiredBks

LISOCIAL2018